Cedric Lawton was born in Manchester in 1943, and was educated at North Manchester Grammar School and the Manchester College of Commerce, where he obtained a Fellowship of the Institute of Export. He worked with ICI and Goodyear, for whom he was Sales Manager in Saudi Arabia, in Jordan, and in Eastern Europe. He now lives in Northern Ireland with his wife and three children.

DOUBLE FIX

CEDRIC LAWTON

THE
BLACKSTAFF
PRESS

BELFAST AND DOVER, NEW HAMPSHIRE

All characters and incidents in this book are fictional, and names have no connection with any person living or dead. Any apparent resemblance is purely coincidental.

First published in 1985
by The Blackstaff Press Limited
3 Galway Park, Dundonald, Belfast BT16 0AN
and
51 Washington Street, Dover, New Hampshire 03820 USA

Printed in Northern Ireland by
The Universities Press Limited

British Library Cataloguing in Publication Data

Lawton, Cedric
Double fix.
I. Title
823'.914[F] *PR6062.A93/*

ISBN 0 85640 335 0 (hardback)
0 85640 329 6 (paperback)

To Rocky Domain
and all involved with him

CHAPTER ONE

Kuwait city, Tuesday April 10th

The lobby of the Sheraton was dimly lit. The men standing at the reception desk had been caught out by a late plane arrival or by the deliberate overbooking system. Their names were registered with the clerk. At two o'clock the rooms reserved by the government would be released for public use and the auction would begin.

The receptionist had one of the most lucrative jobs in the hotel, supplementing his income with the bribes that would be paid to juggle names up and down the list. Five dinars was the going rate to secure a single room, fifteen if it was not to be shared. On good nights, when business was brisk, a free-for-all could develop, bringing the clerk the equivalent of a week's wages in less than an hour.

While foreigners slept in the rooms above, local Arabs sat in the lounge, drinking tea from small glasses. The lobby was a well known meeting place where business and gossip mixed easily.

Sam Aziz entered the hotel unnoticed. He carried his eighteen stones with difficulty, wheezing audibly as he walked to the tea pit. Taking an armchair facing the door, he lowered his huge bulk into the soft upholstery. To his left, Sherif Maktoum from the Bank of Kuwait argued with his procurer, stressing his point with short jabs of a ring-studded finger. Aziz recognised the Gharabally brothers and an official from the Ministry of Finance and wondered what they were plotting.

A frown creased his brow when he failed to spot the man he was supposed to meet. A boy came towards him carrying a china cup and a glass. Aziz took the glass, his hand trembling slightly as the boy poured the tea from a copper pot. He watched the boy return to the pit, then shifted his attention to the reception desk where the clerk haggled with some of the men.

As the minutes passed he became restless. He hated late-night deals with men he did not know or trust, preferring the open lunch arrangement where the food and company were good. This was furtive, though to be expected when Libyans were involved. Libyans – and Irish. He wondered about the connection.

Aziz considered himself a survivor. Born in Karachi, he was used to fighting to keep himself above the poverty line. He had survived the Second World War selling life insurance to British troops about to go to the fronts and later, when the war was over, he sold Rolex watches with Timex movements to the Americans. He had even survived the Kuwaiti authorities when they found him in residence without a permit. Aziz's saving grace was his contacts. Over the years he had made sure that anyone who met him remembered him, and remembered him kindly. A thousand small favours had been repaid with several large ones, enough for him to rent a flat, run a sandwich stall and marry a girl prettier than he deserved.

At fifty-two, overweight and under-exercised, he knew his time was short. Consequently, he devoted every waking minute to the pursuit of making as much money as he could and spending it with the same alacrity on things which made life bearable.

This was the reason he was losing sleep, waiting to meet an Irishman who called himself Taggart.

Shortly after two, the police did their rounds of the hotel to check that no one was using the foyer to sleep in. Aziz showed his identity card and they moved on. The groups of Arabs began to leave, hugging each other in the traditional farewell.

Taggart appeared as the police left. He was a small man, not much more than five feet five, with dark hair swept from front to back exposing a receding hairline. His suit was crumpled and his tie was askew and he walked to the centre of the foyer with a slight limp. Without looking directly at Aziz, he shuffled over, taking a chair opposite the tired and impatient Pakistani.

The rehearsed speech Aziz had prepared froze on his lips as he gazed at the late arrival. Although he towered above the man who had joined him, he felt an instant rush of adrenalin, a reflex reaction to something inherently vile.

'I'm Taggart.'

'Pleased to meet you.'

Taggart ignored the outstretched hand. 'Things have been finalised. The shipment is to go to the Embassy this week. Either Thursday or Friday. We'll phone you tomorrow with the exact details. In exchange for the goods you will be given a driving licence application form already completed and signed. You will bring this to me at the hotel. When I'm satisfied that the form is as expected, you'll be paid.'

Aziz resisted the temptation to laugh. 'Forgive me . . . don't you feel that a great deal of trust is being asked? All that trust seems very one-sided.'

Taggart seemed not to have heard.

'Perhaps,' Aziz continued, 'you fail to realise that I am not alone in this transaction. It is not my trust you are asking, it is that of the supplier. He would hardly agree to such an arrangement.'

Taggart stretched, extending his legs towards Aziz. The Pakistani overcame the urge to draw back. Instead he studied the man before him.

The suit Taggart wore was of a poor cloth and not tailor made. Even allowing for changes in physique it had obviously never been anything but short in the sleeves and tight under the arms. The dirt in the calloused hands might have signified an honest trade in some men but Aziz was sure that this man was unfamiliar with work of any kind. He had seen hands like this on men who had fought in Europe, the dirt so ingrained that no amount of washing could completely remove it. Taggart's shirt collar was frayed and grubby, the result of constant wear. His pale blue eyes were emotionless, staring off into space. Aziz recognised the symptoms. They were those of a man who had spent much of his life fighting, constantly on the run.

With a new appreciation of the situation, he tried again.

Friday April 13th

The sun was sinking low, casting shadows across the souk. The money changers moved their stalls away from the thoroughfare towards the brightly lit offices at the back of the square. Their places were taken by the trinket sellers who shouted their wares from the pavements.

Sam Aziz walked close to the walls. Every now and then ne looked over his shoulder to make sure that Ahmed was following. Ahmed nodded an acknowledgement, a sign that the heavy package dangling from his arm was safe. This was the third time he had been chosen by Aziz for an important mission and although he was unaware of the contents of the parcel he knew that, for twenty dinars payment, it must be important. The work was simple. He was to follow Aziz to the corner of 'Canada Dry' Street where he would hand over the package, then follow his master at a discreet distance. If trouble started – unlikely, Aziz had said – Ahmed would be expected to earn the twenty dinars.

Aziz paused at the tailor's shop to talk to Samir. The shirts had been ordered two weeks ago and a preliminary fitting had been made. Samir smiled as his customer entered the shop, his lips parting to reveal black and cracked teeth. They shook hands, exchanging formal greetings. Aziz refused the tea, choosing a bottle of Coke from the fridge.

'It is a pleasure to see you again,' Samir said. 'Your shirts are nearly ready. A few final touches and the job is done.'

Aziz drained the bottle of Coke. 'Samir, I don't know how you survive. Seven children, two sisters and a wife to support and you seem singularly disinterested in taking my money.'

'Your problem, Mr Aziz, is that you fail to appreciate the individual attention I give to your orders. Every stitch must be perfect, every button must be just so.' He emphasised this by tapping a podgy finger on Aziz's chest. 'You can stay to talk?'

Aziz glanced into the back of the shop where the sweated labour toiled. 'No. I have a meeting.'

'Such a pity.'

'Hurry with the shirts.'

Samir waited until Aziz was lost in the crowd before picking up the phone. His actions were about to lose him a regular customer, but one hundred dinars was ample compensation.

Aziz relaxed as he reached the main street running down to the Sheraton. He took the package from his assistant without a word.

The new arrangements with the Irishman pleased him. He had worked too hard and long on the project to be cheated at the last minute by an Irish/Libyan conspiracy. The package was to be given directly to Taggart in exchange for cash. He had chosen the Sheraton because he knew it would be crowded at this time of day. A simple arrangement, with no chance for Taggart to pull a double-cross. The Irishman could ferry the drugs to the Embassy and Aziz could return to his wife and plan a fresh beginning in his homeland.

His brother had done the job well. The thirty-foot container had arrived safely, its false sides hiding the precious packets of powder. With the connivance of customs officials it had been easy to check the container into the country. The Kuwaitis knew that the cargo was for onward carriage. It was merely in transit and, as such, a perfectly respectable way for people to earn a little extra money.

Now it was nearly over. Half a mile down the street an unlikely associate would be handing over enough cash to keep him in luxury for the rest of his life. He made one last glance to ensure that Ahmed was tailing him and quickened his pace. It never occurred to him that the timing of his journey had played into the Irishman's hands. As the street darkened, men stepped out of the shadows, knives at the ready. Before he could react they were upon him, slashing and cutting. He instinctively turned to look for Ahmed, but his vision clouded. Agonising pain enveloped his body. The last thing he remembered was the sight of a bluish tangle of cords spilling from his shirt. By the time his body hit the pavement he was dead.

CHAPTER TWO

Dublin, Sunday May 6th

Pat Carney raised himself on one elbow, glanced at the clock, remembered it was his day off and breathed a sigh of relief. A watery sun shone through a chink in the curtains and cast a sliver of light across the bed. Outside, a dog was barking and children played in the street.

Carney lay on his back, staring at the cracks in the ceiling. His toes protruded from beneath the sheets and he drew in his feet, shivering in the cold morning air. Before long the problems of his job intruded into his thoughts, making further sleep impossible. As Head of the Garda Drug Squad, he was responsible for a problem that threatened to get out of hand. His hard-pressed unit was in danger of being swamped by a growing workload and his limited budget needed careful management.

At forty-two years of age, with a wife, two children, a dog and a mortgage, he felt he could do without the extra pressures of his job.

He looked at his wife, Mary, sleeping peacefully at his side. Swinging his legs over the edge of the bed, he tiptoed to the bathroom, carefully avoiding the creaking floorboard on the landing.

The reflection staring back at him in the mirror was a disappointment. His hairline was receding and streaks of grey had appeared at the sides. Taking his beaver-haired shaving brush, he lathered his face, scraping off the overnight growth with a safety razor.

All was quiet downstairs. The dog was sleeping by the kitchen door, blocking the entrance, and he stepped over it, hoping it would not waken. He prepared a breakfast of bacon and egg. The dog joined him as he was finishing the last of the rashers. It accepted the bacon from his hand, swallowing the piece whole.

Ten minutes later, his daughter arrived, her long blond hair shining in the sunlight.

'Morning, Daddy.'

'How's my girl today?'

He watched her pour the cereal into a bowl. She was tall for her age, with long legs and an easy walk that quickly covered the ground to the kitchen table.

'Are you going to feed the animal first?'

'Whiskey is not an animal. He's a member of this family.'

The dog stood by Carney's chair, salivating over his slippers. He resisted the urge to kick it. He hated dogs, especially this one.

Mary poked her head round the door. 'You've eaten a full breakfast. I can smell it.'

'It's the weekend.'

'Dieting is banned at weekends?' She made a clucking sound and walked to the sink, eyeing the evidence of the greasy plate.

At thirty-five, she felt she was fast approaching the age when the youngish suddenly became oldish. Carney put his arms round her slim waist.

'Where's Brian?'

Mary shrugged. 'In the bathroom, I suppose. I heard him getting up.'

'What do you want to do today?'

'The beach would be nice.'

Carney considered the idea with initial loathing, changing his mind when he realised it would keep him out of the garden and, more important, away from the telephone.

'Well?'

'Promise you'll stop nagging me?'

She swatted him with a dishcloth. 'If we hurry, we can make ten Mass and go straight from there.'

Three hours later they were on their way, crawling in the traffic on the Dun Laoghaire Road. Brian was there under duress. There were programmes to be written, books to be read, all with the aim of making him the world's greatest computer technician. He sulked in the back seat, ignoring the constant chatter of his twelve-year-old sister.

The beach was crowded. They sat against the breakwater, huddled together on two large towels.

'Pat,' his wife said, when the children were in the water, 'is anything worrying you?'

'Nothing more than usual.'

'You seem very quiet, that's all.'

'You've heard it all before. Not enough hours in the day, not enough cash in the budget, not enough men on the streets. You want me to go on?'

Mary turned over and lay on her stomach. 'Think positive. You might surprise yourself.'

Sinead ran across the sand. 'It's freezing in there.'

Mary tossed her a towel. 'Dry yourself properly and tell Brian not to stay in too long.'

The sun began to sink in the sky and a cooler wind sprang off the sea. 'There has to be a way to stop it,' Mary said.

'The people at the top never handle the drugs. They run the business through a network on the streets.'

'How do they bring the stuff in? Surely they have to be involved then?'

'Not really. The deals are done in Europe, in the Far East, wherever they can find a supplier. They ship it in with couriers, smuggle it in boats, even consign it with legitimate shipping companies, disguised as freight. Their men move it to safe houses and it gets distributed to the pushers. You catch one and all he can give you is the name of another pusher. There are no links to the men at the top. They probably never see it.'

'Can't you arrest the pushers *en masse*?'

'To arrest a pusher, he must be in possession. We haven't the men or the time to mount an operation like that. At any one time, only a small number of pushers will be carrying.'

'Why don't you just shoot the lot of them?'

'I don't have the budget.'

Mary sat up straight. 'We should go soon. It's getting cold.'

Carney went to the water's edge, waving to the children. The white vee of a ship's wake headed out to sea and he felt a momentary pang of envy. The ship was leaving, people were leaving, sailing away from it all.

'Help me with the bags,' Mary called.

Reluctantly he dragged himself to the car.

'What does Walsh say about it?' Mary asked.

'Walsh thinks I'm Superman. As long as I don't shoot myself in the foot, it's okay with him.'

'Tell him you can't cope.'

Carney gave her a jaundiced look. 'Oh yeah, great idea.'

CHAPTER THREE

Dublin, Monday May 21st
Maire Brady huddled close to the wall in an effort to lose herself in the shadows. A couple walked by without a glance, their heads close together, their eyes concentrating on each other.

The girl in the shadows rubbed a hand across her stomach. Waves of nausea threatened to overpower her. Her skin was coated in a clammy sheen of sweat and the cramps, at first infrequent, were becoming one long, drawn-out pain. She had never let it get this far before.

The effect of the cold night air on her damp skin increased her uncontrolled shivering and it crossed her mind that she might be dying. Glancing at her watch for the third time in less than a minute, she willed herself to survive.

A car eased into the kerb and her heart skipped a beat. She watched with relief as it continued down the road, coming to a halt outside the brightly lit entrance to the Shelbourne Hotel. A middle-aged woman climbed out of the back seat, swishing a blue fox fur around her shoulders as the chill wind hit her. The doorman raised an arm in greeting and stepped out, taking the woman by the elbow to escort her up the short steps into the foyer.

Inside the plush reception area, Maire could see groups of people embracing, their faces smiling and animated as they welcomed each other. At the windows of the restaurant, shadowy figures nodded their heads, and through the ventilation grills the smell of hot, rich food wafted into the street.

Maire had begun to die the day she arrived in Dublin. She had been swept along with the crowd, following them without question, enjoying her new-found freedom in the cafes and pubs off O'Connell Street. The unfamiliar faces that accompanied her treated her as one of their own. No demands were made, nothing was expected of her except an empathy with their thoughts and actions. She had accepted the offer of an amphetamine as she would a drink.

The cramming for her arts degree at Trinity College was the catalyst that had propelled her into the world of shadows. She had once looked young for her age. A golden angel, her mother had called her. Now, the glossy hair had metamorphosed into a mass of stringy locks. The once clear eyes were dull – seeing, but rarely appreciating. The brain that had been full of thoughts of success, the bright life and boys, had now developed animal instincts tuned only to survival.

Survival for Maire was dispensed by Jockey. Jockey pushed 'horse'.

Scanning the street for him, she clutched her sides to control the trembling. At her back, the wind rustled the trees and shrubs that formed a protective square around St Stephen's Green. The wrought-iron railings dug into her as she shrank from the traffic prowling for parking spaces. The parking meters stood like sentinels, their slanting shadows marking out boundaries on the cold, stone slabs.

The doors of the Shelbourne swung to and fro, disgorging groups of theatre goers, refreshed and oiled, ready for the short walk to the Gaiety down the road. The constant activity increased her feelings of anxiety, feeding the symptoms of withdrawal. The sights and sounds of the city, once a comfort, now conspired against her in a muddled, alien din.

Finally she could stand it no longer. Holding her coat closed, she ran from the square.

Carney surveyed his wife over the top of the newspaper. 'A holiday?' he asked. He adjusted his position to allow her head to fit comfortably in his lap.

'It strikes me,' she said, 'that we could do with a proper holiday. Somewhere exotic and hard to find, where telephones don't exist.'

'You mean Killarney?'

'I'm serious. Be honest, how many days can you take at one time? We needn't do anything too expensive. Sinead's going to

France with the school and Brian will be in Scotland for the whole of the summer holidays. It's an ideal opportunity.'

'What about the dog? Where's he going this summer? Your mother won't have him.'

'If it's only the dog between me and a proper holiday I'll shoot the damn thing and tell the children it ran off.'

'We'll see.'

Mary stretched out her arm and felt under the cushion. 'I was at the shops yesterday. I picked these up on the way back.'

Reluctantly he took the brochures from her hand and flicked through the pages. Here and there he paused, lingering over the resorts picturing topless bathers.

'The prices are reasonable if you pick the month carefully,' Mary prompted.

'More reasonable than what?'

'More reasonable than the two of us staying here when the children are away. I don't understand what you have against holidays. You weren't always like this.'

He wanted to give her a reasoned explanation but he did not understand it himself. It was easy to blame the job, but others managed it each year. He liked travelling, especially if it involved flying, and he even enjoyed the change of diet. It was the tension, he thought bitterly. At the station and out on the streets he could work it off. Sitting on a beach under a blistering sun, the tension grew.

'I'll see what the arrangements are.'

Mary turned her head away to watch the television.

Later, Carney stood at the front door waiting patiently for the dog as it urinated on his roses. The sky was clear and dotted with clusters of twinkling stars. Over the rooftops he could see the glow from the city and his thoughts went back to the streets and alleyways. Ignoring the dog sniffing at his feet, he took a deep breath and wished it was morning.

Jockey leaned back against the wall, surveying the flow of people up and down O'Connell Street. The poise of an hour ago was swiftly vanishing. The man who made others wait had been stood up for the second time this evening. It was rare for one of his users to miss an appointment and unheard of for two not to show. It was also dangerous. It meant he would be stuck with two packets of heroin. He half considered going back to the previous drop, thinking a traffic problem might be holding them up. The late-night buses rumbled in with their passengers at regular intervals and he dismissed the idea. Years on the street had given him an instinct for trouble and this was trouble in a big way. Zipping up his suede jacket, he turned in the direction of the Liffey, walking near the kerb, ready to run at the first sight of a Drug Squad patrol.

As he hurried over the bridge, he remembered that this had happened once before, in the early days of the business. When competition had come to town.

CHAPTER FOUR

Dublin, Tuesday May 22nd

The rain slanted diagonally across Harcourt Street, fragmenting as it hit the pavement. Detective Inspector Carney quickened his pace as the offices of the Drug Squad came into sight. Dodging his fellow pedestrians and ducking his head to avoid the scything umbrellas, he hugged the wall at every opportunity.

Inside, the offices were warm and the heavy doors shut out the sounds of wind and rain.

'Morning, Sergeant,' Carney said as he paused to let the heat penetrate his bones.

'Morning, sir,' Sergeant Fitzgerald replied, without raising his head from the heavy ledger that dominated the reception desk. 'The Superintendent called.'

'How did he sound?'

'Like someone had put a ferret down his trousers.'

'I'm glad he was in a good mood. Any message?'

'Nothing he would trust me with.'

Carney and Fitzgerald were old friends. They had started the Drug Squad some fifteen years earlier in a cramped office in Dublin Castle. Just the two of them and a girl to do the typing. In a way, their expansion and the move to the new offices to give them more room testified to the growing problem and Carney's constant requests for more staff indicated that he might be losing the battle.

Carney walked to his desk, tossing the sodden raincoat onto the straight-backed chair in the corner of the office. He grimaced as he recognised the folder containing the overtime sheets and consigned them to the pending tray with a sweep of his hand. Eyeing the other papers on his desk suspiciously, he manipulated a bunch of keys with one hand, selecting and inserting the right one into the top drawer.

'Daly,' he called.

Daly heard the summons. Folding his morning paper, he ran a hand through his thick, black, wiry hair, straightened his tie and dutifully poked his head into Carney's office.

'Am I doing anything today?' Carney inquired.

'You're addressing a parent/teacher meeting this afternoon. I've dug out your notes and left them in the tray. And McQuillan called. Wants to speak to you about the Ryan case.'

'What about the Ryan case?'

Daly shrugged. 'Didn't say. Just for you to call back as soon as you came in.'

Carney gazed at the Sergeant, wondering whether the sharply creased trousers and stylish jacket were tailor made. 'Give these to Liam,' he said, motioning towards the files, 'and bring me the morning papers if they've arrived.'

When Daly had gone he reached into a drawer and took out a photograph of his wife and children. He placed it at an angle to the light to avoid a glare from the glossy surface. It was his favourite family snapshot. The children had their arms around their mother and were smiling at the camera. He remembered the day it was taken. One of those rare, balmy days when the temperature was just right, the birds were singing and all the bills had been paid. Shadows from the cherry tree fell across the group, adding an artistic touch which he insisted was deliberate. His wife looked happy then. Really happy.

'Liam,' he said, picking up the phone. 'Get me McQuillan at the Prosecutor's office.'

He held on, listening to the ethereal noises as the connection was made.

'Mike,' he said when the voice answered, 'how are you today?'

'Good morning, Patsy. Thanks for calling. I'm fine.'

Carney pictured the ruddy face behind the disembodied voice. Mike McQuillan was another contemporary, having started at the Bar before moving into the Director of Prosecutions office. He was a rugby nut, but otherwise dependable.

'I wanted to talk to you about the Ryan case,' McQuillan continued. 'I've read the file through again and I don't see any mention of a struggle.'

'Struggle?' Carney repeated dully. 'What bloody struggle?'

'I was hoping you'd say that. It appears our Mr Ryan paraded a bruised left eye in front of his defence counsel on Friday night, claiming it happened at the station.'

'At the Bridewell?' Carney exploded.

'No, not at the Bridewell. Claims he was assaulted by the arresting officer.'

'Christ!'

'Thought you might like to investigate this carefully in the circumstances. After the recent spate of cock-ups it would be as well.'

Carney felt sick. They had been staking out Ryan for a week. 'I take it he's accusing Daly?'

'Hasn't named him, but I suppose so if he made the arrest.'

'Let me talk to Daly and I'll get back to you.'

They said perfunctory farewells and Carney resisted the urge to slam the receiver into the cradle. Instead, he closed his eyes and tried to conjure up visions of topless bathers on a Spanish beach.

Across the city, in a modest detached house opposite Griffith Park, the curtains were being pulled back. The face that greeted the miserable morning was lined and surrounded with a blue-black stubble sprouting from a square jaw. The eyes, that narrowed to slits to shut out the light, were bloodshot and the overall appearance was of a man who was not pleased to be facing a new day. Brendan Rafferty rubbed his fingers through his heavy overnight growth and listened to the sounds from the kitchen. A faint smell of something frying reached his nostrils, sending unwelcomed messages to his stomach.

In the kitchen his sister-in-law, Rose, busied herself at the stove. She smiled as she worked, conscious of the fact they would be suffering from hangovers.

Her husband, Sean, was the first to brave the offer of a meal. At thirty-five, he was rapidly going to seed. Heavy bags beneath his eyes testified to a succession of late nights and intemperate drinking.

'How did it go?' Rose asked.

'Well enough.'

Rose ladled an egg onto his plate, adding a well cooked piece of bacon.

'Anyone there I know?'

'No one you'd be sorry to miss.'

Brendan edged away from the door, collapsing into an armchair at the far end of the living room. As he recovered slightly, his mind wrestled with the problems of why his pushers were wandering about Dublin with a quarter of the dope still in their pockets. He had been supplying the market for over fifteen years and there was no one he could think of who would be stupid enough to muscle in on his business.

Sean joined him. 'Did you find out anything last night?' Brendan asked.

'More or less the same all over. Two or three users failing to show. I talked to Flanagan's man. He was having the same trouble. Lots of panicky pushers wanting to know what to do.'

Brendan lit a cigarette. 'I don't want any misunderstandings. Is that clear? We'll play it nice and cool. Put some men on the street. Ask some questions.'

Sean nodded. 'It has to be a fairly big supply. Twenty-two junkies missing in twelve hours. Could be a one-off.'

'Smells bad. But then everything smells bad this morning.'

Maire Brady tried hard to control her trembling. Jockey circled her, like a farmer looking over a specimen of prize beef. She felt his eyes wandering over her body and fought the desire to be sick.

'You know what it's like?' he asked, the packet of white powder just out of reach. 'It's a bad scene. You'd do anything, just anything if I made you wait long enough.'

Maire turned her face to the wall, her cheek pressed against the hard, cold stone. Tears trickled down her face.

'You'd do things you can't even imagine.'

Maire felt dizzy. A sensation crept over her as if she were leaving her body and gazing down at two strangers.

'With a body like yours, all the worries could disappear. No more lying or stealing. All the dope you could use.'

The white packet came into view and despite herself she turned, her hand reaching out.

'Oh, no,' Jockey said, snatching the packet away. 'You have to want it so badly you'd beg for it. That will take a little time yet.'

Maire watched in horror as the heroin was withdrawn. A rage built up, a blind rage that swept aside the nausea and pain.

'I don't need you,' she heard herself say. 'There are plenty of others now. I don't need you.'

Jockey grabbed her by the shoulder. 'I know someone who'd like to talk to you.'

Daly drew up his chair to the edge of the desk, half an inch of white cuff showing beneath each sleeve. His hair was neatly groomed, and in his dark suit he looked more like a businessman about to sell his wares than a junior officer facing a pensive boss.

'I spoke to McQuillan,' Carney said. 'Or rather he spoke to me about Ryan.'

'Ryan?'

'Nothing I should know, is there?'

'You saw the report. I gave you the file the following morning.'

'I saw the file. I didn't see Ryan. He says you hit him.'

'That's not true.' Daly brushed the sleeve of his jacket, his eyes avoiding Carney's. 'You know what it's like. He wasn't too pleased when we arrested him. Made a few protests, generally dragged his feet. I might have pushed him.'

'You might have?' Carney said, raising his voice. 'Did he resist arrest?'

'No . . . not exactly.'

'What then?'

Daly bit the inside of his lip. 'Look. Nothing happened. I pushed him into the car. That's all.'

'Go on.'

'I sat in the back. Durcan drove us. We brought him in, held him for a while in the cell and then transferred him to the Bridewell.'

'Who took him down to the cells?'

'I did. Then I came back to the front desk.'

Carney flicked at a pencil with his finger, watching as it rattled across the desk. 'How long was he in the cell before you picked him up?'

'Thirty . . . maybe forty minutes. No longer than that.'

'You were alone when you went for him?'

Daly hesitated. 'Yes.'

'And he didn't give you any trouble?'

'No! Look, it doesn't make any sense. Why would I hit him?'

Carney stretched, feeling the tension growing in the muscles of his legs. A steady throbbing above his eyes heralded another headache and he pushed himself to his feet unsteadily.

'You know,' he said, walking to the filing cabinet, where a silver kettle gleamed in the overhead light, 'this department needs results badly. We have an overtime bill that makes the Commissioner throw up everytime he sees me. Because of that, they watch us like a hawk. If Ryan goes screaming brutality from the rooftops . . . '

'I didn't hit him.'

Carney pushed the plug into the wall socket and stared at his reflection in the polished kettle. The curved side elongated his features and he turned away.

'Let Fitzgerald know where to contact you.' He breathed deeply as the door clicked shut. Daly could have admitted it and made an excuse, he thought as he poured the boiling water into the cup. At least it would have made some kind of sense. He pressed the button on the intercom.

'You called?' Fitzgerald said, his smile fading as he caught sight of Carney's face.

'Sit down Sergeant and help yourself. It's just boiled. There's sugar in the top drawer if you want it.'

'Problems?'

Carney put the mug on his blotter. 'You were on duty when Ryan was brought in. Tell me what happened.'

'Ryan came in with Durcan and Daly. He was taken down to the cells. I phoned the Bridewell to let them know he was on the way.'

'Did he walk in or was he dragged?'

Fitzgerald frowned. 'As far as I remember he was handcuffed to Daly. They all walked in together.'

'Did Ryan make any sort of complaint to you?'

'He wasn't very co-operative, if that's what you mean. He was cursing and swearing . . .'

'You didn't see any marks on his face?'

Fitzgerald took a tentative sip from the cup and sneaked a glance at the Inspector over the rim. 'No. No marks.'

'And you gave Daly the key to take him to the cell?'

'Durcan took the key, gave me the cell number and I logged it.'

'Who took him down?'

'I don't know. I assume it was Durcan. He had the key.'

'But you can't be sure?'

Fitzgerald blew on the surface of the coffee. 'I take it our friend is making some sort of accusation. Perhaps if you tell me what's supposed to have happened I can be of more help.'

'The bastard's black and blue and threatening to cause all sorts of trouble.'

'And he says . . .'

'He says the arresting officer was responsible.'

'Daly?'

'Daly.'

'And where is this supposed to have happened?'

'It was supposed to have happened here.'

Fitzgerald stared at the wall. 'You'd make me feel better,' Carney continued, 'if you denied it violently.'

'You'd sooner I protested too much?'

'When Ryan was brought up for transfer, you saw him again?'

'Durcan came to the desk with the details. Ryan and Daly were in the background.'

'Shit!' Carney sighed. 'Why don't you simply admit you didn't see him?'

'I saw him walk to the door. He wasn't moaning, staggering or complaining. He probably banged his head on the wall in the Bridewell and waited for the swelling to come up.'

Carney sniffed. 'Difficult to bang your eye on a wall. Or anything else for that matter.'

'What does McQuillan say?'

'McQuillan simply wants the facts. If the hard evidence is there, we can brazen it out and take our chances with the publicity.'

'Daly is a steady sort,' Fitzgerald said. 'Not the type to go duffing up the prisoners for no reason.'

'Exactly what I was thinking. That makes it all the worse.'

'How do you mean?'

'We've been after Ryan for how long . . . six months, seven? The whole department has been involved. Everyone knew how important it was to grab him. He's one of Brendan Rafferty's right-hand men. The link between the family and the supplies. Just to have him off the street is a bonus. So why should a conscientious, intelligent officer, who is well aware of the situation, jeopardise all the work that's been put in by hitting him for no good reason?'

'The simple answer is, he didn't touch him.'

'I don't believe you can give yourself a black eye, so it follows that someone gave it to him. Ryan says it was Daly. He had the opportunity.'

'What does Durcan say?'

'I haven't had the chance to speak to him yet, but I imagine he'll have the same story as Daly. From what I can gather, Durcan wasn't alone with Ryan.'

'Okay. Let's say Daly hit him. Why?'

'He wasn't causing any trouble in the cell. Daly said so himself. Daly wasn't personally involved with Ryan. He was just another name to him.'

'No motive.'

'Ryan must have thought it was Christmas when Daly hit him.'

'What are you suggesting?'

'I'm not suggesting anything. Just looking at it from all angles.'

'For God's sake!' Fitzgerald was becoming exasperated. 'If Daly wanted to do Ryan a favour, he wouldn't have arrested him in the first place.'

'Not that simple. Durcan was with him. He had to make a move. If he was to be arrested it might as well be by someone who could help out.'

'Jesus, that's some theory.'

'We have some time. He's been remanded for seven days.

Depends on what his solicitor does in the meantime. If he goes ahead with the complaint there'll be a full enquiry. I want the files of all the cases worked on by Daly since he's been with us, including the ones he's on now. Have them on my desk first thing after lunch and keep this to yourself. I don't want a word of this in the office.'

Fitzgerald finished his coffee in one gulp and stood up. 'I think you're wrong.'

'Let's hope so.'

As Fitzgerald closed the door behind him, Carney considered his options. The last thing he needed was doubts about one of his men. The department was balanced on a knife edge, with everyone watching their progress. The overtime was only tolerated as long as there was a glimmer of hope in the battle against the problems sweeping the city. If further attention was drawn for the wrong reasons, it would all come falling on his head.

Whatever the decision, he would have to watch Daly closely in the future.

CHAPTER FIVE

Amsterdam, Tuesday May 22nd

Abdul Malek glinted in the corner of the restaurant, the gold rings on his fingers catching the light from the massive chandelier in the centre of the dining room. There were still very few people about. Most of the tourists were resting after a long day on the banks of the canals, and the low life would not emerge for a few more hours. One or two businessmen were taking an evening meal before venturing out to sample the diverse and uncensored night life and they kept to themselves.

Malek sat with his back to the wall, diagonally opposite the entrance. He sipped disinterestedly at his lukewarm tea, lamenting its weakness and lack of flavour. The waiters lounged about, only coming to life at the sight of a crooked finger.

Although Malek had never met him, he instantly recognised the scruffy, shambling figure that paused briefly at the door. Smiling broadly, but giving the merest of waves, he caught the man's eye and watched as the figure shuffled towards his table.

As the man neared the chair, Malek half rose from his seat, his hand extended.

'Mr Taggart. A pleasure to meet you.'

Taggart barely touched the outstretched hand. 'You have been in Amsterdam long?'

Taggart nodded briefly, dismissing the waiter who had followed him to the table.

'You do not wish to eat? Some tea perhaps . . . or coffee?'

'I haven't much time,' Taggart said after surveying the restaurant. 'I hear you want to set up another delivery.'

'I understand that our previous arrangement was mutually beneficial. I see no reason to discontinue.'

Taggart studied the brown-faced man who wore too much gold.

The face gave little away but he recognised more of the businessman than the revolutionary in the fine features and well trimmed moustache.

'I thought you had a problem,' said Taggart.

'Problem? What problem is this?'

'You lost your London Embassy.'

Malek laughed too loudly, attracting glances from the surrounding tables. 'We used the Embassy for the first delivery, but it is not essential. We have many ways to help you.'

'The attraction was,' Taggart continued, 'that the Embassy was foolproof. No one can search a diplomatic bag. It was guaranteed. You know how much we need discretion.'

Malek began to unwrap the cellophane from a packet of cigars. He offered one to Taggart. Taggart shook his head.

'We need two, possibly three more deliveries and then we finish. We can't afford to stir up vested interests. That's not the object.'

'I understand, I understand,' Malek assured him. 'We have the set-up. All you have to do is take it across the border into the South.'

'We would prefer delivery in Dublin.'

Malek peered disdainfully at the wooden toothpicks in the small jar at his elbow, rejecting them in favour of a goose quill which he extracted from his top pocket. Covering his mouth with his left hand, he worked away at his teeth, his eyes never leaving Taggart's face. 'We thought it would be a simple matter for you.'

'How would you get the stuff into Belfast?' Taggart asked.

'No problem. Everyone thinks that security on flights to and from Belfast is tight. To a certain extent this is true, but it is all geared towards the arms and explosives. You could carry the poppy fields of Asia in on a camel. They would not be looking for it. We use only legitimate travellers. Businessmen, even the odd clergyman. The body search on arrival is very rare.'

'And Dublin?'

'Dublin is different. The flights are more conspicuous, the customs people more attentive. We could do it, but the risk would be greater.'

'And the method?'

'The method *we* will worry about. All you have to do is arrange for one of your people to meet the courier. The changeover is made at the airport. Safer for all of us.'

'The price?'

'Different from last time of course. Last time it was courtesy of the government. A nominal charge to cover certain costs. For Belfast it would be the price of the goods plus two thousand pounds.'

Although the expression on Taggart's face did not change, Malek was disturbed by the activity that showed in the man's eyes. He had thought that Taggart had a drink problem. The eyes took too much time to focus. Now suddenly they seemed sharp and penetrating and they were concentrating on him. Malek looked away, pretending to attract the attention of a waiter.

'I have good contacts in this city,' Malek said, abruptly changing the subject. 'If there is anything you need during your stay, anything at all, you only have to let me know.'

'I have good contacts too,' Taggart replied in an even tone.

The chair suddenly felt uncomfortable and Malek adjusted his position. 'This is business,' he said. 'If you do not like the arrangements you can go elsewhere.'

Taggart slowly shook his head. 'This is politics. Didn't they tell you that?'

The waiter arrived and hovered over the two men, his pencil poised. 'Some tea,' Malek told him without enthusiasm.

The meeting was not going the way he had expected. Malek had assumed he would be dealing with a reasonable man who understood how these deals worked. All his life he had been in politics, and the one thing he had learnt was that it cost money for a favour. Governments paid in kind. This rat-bag of a man, representing some collective lunacy, was not a politician. Even the crazy men in Tripoli must have realised that.

'Mr Taggart,' he said, 'I realise that this mutual co-operation is to further our respective ideological struggles, but you must understand my position. There are certain expenses over and above those officially recognised by my government. These have to be covered. It is quite normal.'

He eased himself back in the chair, allowing the waiter to place the silver teapot on the table. 'I am not a rich man, Mr Taggart.'

He watched as Taggart lowered his gaze to the array of rings on his fingers. A sudden thirst made him move the offending hand to the teapot and when he finished pouring, the hand disappeared into his trouser pocket.

'Maybe we can do it for less,' Malek offered, knowing that his position was not strong. If they discovered he was taking money on the side he would be posted back to Tripoli, or dropped off on the way, from a great height. 'It is not something that we should allow to stand in the way of our causes.'

'We'll go through Belfast,' Taggart said simply.

The restaurant began to fill. Malek was relieved when Taggart refused his offer to see him to the door. As he watched him go, he fervently wished that the next deal would be far away from Amsterdam. His only consolation was that there had been none of the double-crossing and political chicanery that had turned the Kuwait arrangement into a bloodbath.

Two hours later, with a bare-breasted waitress offering him the bar tariff of the Dante Club, he loosened his tie and tried to relax. The strain of mouthing the right political views in the Embassy, coupled with avoiding his fellow diplomats at night, was taking a heavy toll on his nerves. Ordering a large gin and tonic, he settled back to survey the show. It was the fourth time in a month he had ventured out and, being conservative by nature, he stuck to the places he knew well. The knife edge was becoming sharper by the week and it would soon be necessary to cash in the Zurich account and join his fellow exiles. Cursing Taggart in his native tongue, he hid in the subdued lighting, mentally making plans for his escape.

Dublin, Tuesday May 22nd

'Jesus!' Sean Rafferty muttered, bending over the writhing figure. 'How long has she been like this?'

'Just the right length of time,' Jockey replied, secretly amused by Rafferty's discomfort. It would do the bastard good to see the result of his business.

'Can she talk?'

'Oh yes, she can talk,' Jockey said, flicking his half-finished cigarette into the darkness of the waste ground.

A steady drizzle enveloped them and Rafferty cursed. 'Get on with it then.'

Jockey moved to one side and grabbed the girl by her arm, tugging her to her feet. He gripped the damp cloth of her coat, supporting and threatening her at the same time. Slapping her once across the face, he drew her close, his mouth pressed against her ear. 'There's someone here to see you Maire,' he whispered. 'Someone you'd do well to help.'

He moved his head back a fraction, staring into the girl's eyes to make sure she was paying attention. 'You can put a stop to this agony Maire. Just give me the name.'

Maire's head rolled to one side. 'I don't know his name,' she answered in a whisper. 'He came to the disco. Afterwards he was outside.'

'What did he say?' Jockey prompted, squeezing tightly on her arm.

'Nothing!' she cried. 'He was just selling.'

'And you bought?'

'You hadn't shown up. I was desperate.'

'What did he look like?'

Jockey slapped her again, using the back of his hand. The ring on his finger caught her below the eye. Blood began to trickle down her cheek, mixing with the tears. Jockey loosened his grip and allowed her to slide.

'Stay with her,' Sean said. 'And don't call me out unless you have some concrete information.'

Jockey glanced down as the arm encircled his leg. Maire clung on with what little strength she had left, afraid he would leave her there. Jockey stooped, grabbing a handful of hair. As he pulled her to her feet she vomited over his shoes.

CHAPTER SIX

Dublin, Friday May 25th

The forecourt and the ground-floor corridors of the flats smelled like an open sewer, the younger inhabitants of the sprawling complex preferring to relieve themselves where they played rather than climb the staircases to their homes on the higher levels. A number of feral cats scrounged a living in the building, competing for space on the darkened landings with the graffiti scrawlers and the winos who bedded down for the night.

Mad Johnny, his thinning hair waving in the wind, dragged himself up the first flight of concrete steps. Inside, he felt a mixture of rage and despair. Every week he attended the Tenants Association meeting and every week he listened to the same catalogue of misery. They talked in circles, crying on each other's shoulders, but nothing was ever done. The lifts were still out of order, the central-heating system froze them in the winter and suffocated them in the summer. Muggings were rife and nearly every flat on the first three levels had shattered doors where the boots of marauding vandals had smashed them off their locks.

At sixty years of age and with a failing heart, Mad Johnny took the climb slowly. Since his wife died, a vital spark had gone out of his life. To compensate he had organised the association. The committee of six met each Friday night, using their apartments on a strict rotation. The discussions rarely lasted more than an hour, partly because Johnny always took the chair and refused to tolerate unnecessary chatter and partly because it ate into his available drinking time.

His fingers trembled as he inserted the key in the lock. The inside of the flat was a mess. Dinner dishes shared the table with breakfast bowls, and clothes were strewn about the furniture.

Lowering himself on the threadbare couch, he lay back, his

hands covering his face. A more sinister complaint had surfaced during their latest meeting, one which made him shake with rage. Mrs Lennon's daughter had been found on the fifth-floor landing, her eyes glazed, blood pouring from her arm where the needle had punctured the vein. It was the first time an incident of this nature had touched them closely, but they knew it was a growing problem throughout the block. The calls for action had been wild. A posse of vigilantes had been suggested and someone had even considered calling in the Garda. In the end, the debate had deteriorated to such an extent that there was a danger of them coming to blows. The association was falling apart. He had to do something to revive it.

The tattered green book of telephone numbers was inches from his hand. He reached out until his fingers were almost touching the scuffed cover. He hesitated, uncertain of what he would say to his brother-in-law. To calm his nerves, he paced the carpet, glancing out of the window every few steps to look at the sky.

He was painfully aware of his nickname of Mad Johnny. It was a legacy from the days when his drinking was out of control. If he took the matter of the pushers into his own hands and anything went wrong he would be subject to further torment from his neighbours.

As he increased his pace he thought of Nial Devlin and what he represented. Nial had married his sister in the early seventies and shortly after had joined the IRA. Nial was back in Dublin, living less than two miles from the flats, and Johnny saw him in the local pub every once in a while. They talked of horses, another of Johnny's failings, but in the background there was always the spectre of Nial's activities in the North.

Wandering to the kitchen, he opened the cupboard door above the sink and took out the bottle of Powers. He poured a generous measure into a plastic cup and swallowed it in one gulp. The liquid burned his throat, making him cough and he bent forward, an arm outstretched to steady himself against the sink.

As the whiskey calmed his stomach, he felt a brief period of elation and a certainty that he was right. The pushers were a menace, preying on the young and the weak, drawing them into the trap until there was no escape.

Flicking through the pages, he found Nial's number. He picked up the phone and dialled, his breathing heavy as he heard the purr of the ringing tone.

'Nial?'

The voice at the other end had a soft lilt that never failed to warm him.

'I wonder if I could see you? There's a problem . . . No, I'm okay . . . I could explain better when we meet.'

Johnny picked up a pencil from the table and jotted down an address. 'Yes. I think I can find it. Thanks . . . I'll see you.'

Breathing a sigh of relief, he dropped the receiver into the cradle and reached for his coat.

The house stood on a corner, a light showing through a crack in the downstair curtains. Johnny paused at the gate, looking over his shoulder for no good reason. Taking a deep breath, he tried to control the nerves fluttering in his stomach.

Nial answered his knock, greeting him with a smile and a slap on the shoulder. Johnny allowed the younger man to take his coat and followed him to a room at the back where a fire was burning in the grate.

'Must be three or four weeks since I saw you,' Nial said.

Johnny nodded in agreement, easing himself into an armchair under the window. 'Not as fit as I was,' he said. 'It's the heart. Does it no good climbing those steps every day.'

'Why doesn't someone fix the lifts? Can't that organisation of yours arrange it?'

'We've complained till we're blue in the face but they've given up on us. As soon as they fix it, some bastards come and cut the wires again. Same with most things at the flats.'

'Can't they move you down a bit? Ask for a change or a transfer?'

'You think I haven't tried? Trouble is, everyone's name is on the list. They can't move us all.'

'Guinness okay?'

Johnny nodded. As Nial disappeared into the kitchen, he leaned forward to warm his hands at the fire.

'Watch it,' Nial said, handing him a glass filled to the brim. 'You said you had a problem.'

Johnny sipped through the froth and set the glass on the mantelpiece. 'Not my problem really. It's the pushers. They're causing a lot of trouble.'

'Pushers at the flats?'

'They're crawling all over the place. The kids don't stand a chance. The Drug Squad can't be there all the time. They make a raid every so often but the pushers just lie low for a few days until it blows over. Any that get arrested are replaced overnight. That's why I thought you might be able to help.'

'Me?'

'Through your contacts.'

'I don't think . . .'

'We can't do anything about it ourselves. Too many of them and they're backed by heavies. A girl was found half dead on one of the landings. Daughter of a friend of mine. She was doped up to the eyeballs. Only a youngster, fifteen or sixteen. The family are a good sort, no problems . . . they do their best for the children and then these pieces of shit walk in and ruin their lives.'

Nial shook his head.

'Just a frightener,' said Johnny. 'Something to scare them off. If they think the IRA are protecting the flats they'll think twice about it. I know they'll go somewhere else but it gives us a chance. You can keep children in at nights.'

'We don't act as vigilantes.'

'I'm not asking for a permanent presence. Just one incident so we can put the word about.' Johnny rubbed his hand over his face. His bones were aching from the walk to the house and he suddenly felt tired.

Nial took his glass to the kitchen, returning with an open bottle. 'Pour your own,' he said.

Johnny sipped the dark liquid. 'When we formed the association we were approached by Sinn Fein. We didn't work with them because we didn't want to get involved with politics. But . . . I'm sure we could reconsider.'

There was silence for a moment. Johnny shifted in his seat,

feeling uncomfortable under Nial's steady gaze. He wanted to tell his brother-in-law that it was violence that worried him, but the words stuck in his throat.

'I'll talk to my people,' Nial said. 'You won't hear anything from us but you'll know if it happens.'

Johnny felt his stomach lurch. 'We don't want any killing.'

'Don't worry about it. We know what to do.'

CHAPTER SEVEN

Dublin, Saturday May 26th
'Not bad,' Carney said, holding the poster at arms length. 'It has just the right amount of morbid fascination.'

Daly cocked his head, pondering the print of a corpse being carried away on a stretcher, the legend HEROIN MAKES THE GOING EASY written in red beneath a trailing, lifeless arm.

'Where will you put it?' Daly asked, hoping it would not be in his office.

'I thought we'd put it in reception. Fitzgerald appreciates fine art.'

Carney rolled the poster up, sliding the elastic band into place. Taking Daly's raincoat from the back of a chair, he tossed it to him.

'Where to?' Daly asked.

'Callaghan's.'

Carney swept through the doors, Daly trailing behind, one arm flailing as he struggled with the coat.

'A present for you,' Carney said, sliding the poster along the top of the reception desk. 'Stick it somewhere prominent and don't draw any moustaches on it.'

Before Fitzgerald could react he was outside, his head slanted towards the leaden sky. It had rained just enough to make the roads slick and greasy.

'You drive,' he said, offering the keys to Daly.

Callaghan's Disco sprawled above the ground-floor offices of a coal importer. The staircase up to the gold-tinted glass doors was lined with garish pictures of pop stars whose names Carney could not begin to guess. He rang the bell, admiring the golden entrance. He thought of a trip he had once made on the canals of Amsterdam. The tour had taken them out into the port where the Shell Building dominated the landscape, its sides a solid rank of gold-tinted glass. Seven ounces in the whole structure, he remembered, wondering if Callaghan's glass contained the real thing.

Callaghan opened the doors, a sallow face peering out at them.

'You don't seem pleased to see me,' Carney observed as he brushed past, not waiting for an invitation.

Callaghan followed them, scratching the back of his neck. He wore an open-necked shirt, crumpled at the collar, and was smoking a black cheroot, the smell of which hung about the room in a thick, cloying pall. The belt at his waist had been loosed, allowing the black trousers to almost hide the glossy pointed shoes. Self-consciously, he hitched them up, tightening the belt by a notch.

'Strange life you must lead,' Carney remarked, taking a stool from the bar. 'Living in the dark, working in the dark. You don't disintegrate in the sun's rays, do you?'

Callaghan gave an artificial smile as he ducked under the counter. 'I don't suppose you want a drink?'

'Wouldn't mind a coffee. One for you too, Sergeant?'

Callaghan sighed heavily. 'Maeve,' he shouted through the curtain which separated the bar from a small kitchen, 'make up a pot will you?'

There was no reply, but they heard a tap running followed by the unmistakable sounds of water splashing into a kettle.

'Can't be fire regulations,' Callaghan said, fishing for a reason for their visit.

'Wrong department,' Carney informed him, pausing to gaze around the dimly lit room. 'God, it must be hell in here.'

'The kids like it,' Callaghan protested.

'Kids like all sorts of things that aren't good for them.'

Daly climbed onto a stool next to Carney. 'Bet the decibel level in here breaks a few noise abatement regulations.'

'Wrong department,' Callaghan said in disgust. 'What is it you want? I have to clean up and get home.'

'We hear the pushers are using this place to make their contacts,' said Carney casually.

'Oh come on. Don't give me that shit. I'd break their necks if I found any of them in here. I can't watch everything that goes on. There are 200 kids in here some nights. They could be testing Cruise missiles for all I know.'

'You must notice the results,' Daly said.

'What the hell's that supposed to mean?'

'Glassy eyes, unco-ordinated movements, bodies flaked out over the tables,' Daly prompted. 'You must have noticed.'

'I don't want any trouble. It's bad enough as it is. Where do they train you? Since when have discos been a social evil?'

'We don't want any trouble either,' Carney said, his eyes brightening as the coffee arrived. 'Thank you Maeve. We were just asking your husband if he noticed anyone pushing drugs last night.'

Maeve shook her long, red hair, gathering it in her hands and sweeping it over her shoulders. 'We don't allow them in,' she answered, cocking her head to one side as she studied Daly.

'So you know who they are?' said Carney.

Callaghan sighed. After eight hours of flashing lights and deafening noise, he was in no mood for this. 'Look, Inspector, I'm not responsible for what they pass to each other under the table. You're the law around here. Why don't you search anyone you suspect at the door? You make it sound as if I'm in business with them.'

'Seen Brendan Rafferty lately?' Daly asked.

'No law against having friends, is there?'

Carney asked Maeve for another coffee. 'Must be a worry running this place,' he said. 'Wiring, fire hazards . . . is the door to the fire escape locked?'

Callaghan stared at him coldly. They sat in silence for a while waiting for the fresh coffee.

'We don't expect names and addresses,' Daly said as Maeve placed the cups on the counter.

'I've nothing to tell you.'

Carney pushed the cup to one side. 'I'll finish it later.'

Callaghan watched them go and spat in the sink.

Outside in the fresh air, Carney took a deep breath. Perhaps he had judged Daly too harshly, he thought, as he climbed into the car. The Sergeant handled himself well and there was obviously no awkwardness in his conversation with Callaghan.

'Do you think we should put a man in there tonight?'

Carney smiled. 'Not on overtime. On the other hand, if a certain sergeant wanted to make amends and have a scout round in his own time . . .'

The steady, pulsating throb filtered its way down the street, drawing the dancers to it like a moth to the light. They came in all colours and sizes, wrapped up in their own private worlds.

As with all mass gatherings, the predators lurked in the shadows, watchful, stealthy, seeking out the weakest. It was not hard for them to spot their prey. They looked for the anxious face, the frightened eyes, the little gestures that marked them apart from the others.

Tonight, however, the hunters themselves were being stalked. Simon Toman watched as the boy moved in and out of the crowd. Toman's eyes never left his victim for a moment. He had first spotted him on the steps outside. It took one to know one. There was an intruder on his patch and action was necessary.

The boy knew the risk he was taking. He kept close to the walls, constantly on the move, watching for signs of trouble. In the end it was the girl who sought him out. A pretty face peered into his own, the anxious look in her eyes asking the question. He showed her a glimpse of the packet and money was thrust into his hand. It was over in a second and he relaxed. It was his first mistake.

He made his way down the crowded stairway, pausing on the street. A car pulled up, all four doors opening quickly. He started to move to his left and found his path blocked. A youth about his own age placed a hand on his shoulder. Then there were other hands, pressing his head down, dragging him into the car. He felt himself being forced into the seat as the car accelerated away. As the crowded city retreated into the fading light, the thought crossed his mind that he might never see it again.

Daly was dressed out of character. Gone were the neatly pressed trousers and stylish jacket. In their place he wore a pair of old jeans, a faded orange shirt, a thin denim jacket and a pair of casual shoes. His hair was combed forward in a quiff and his shirt was open at the neck.

Mounting the stairs two at a time, he lost himself in the smoky atmosphere of the disco. It took some time for the aural and visual shock to wear off. He watched the girls gyrating on the dancefloor, their hair tumbling and cascading as they shook their heads in time to the music. He found it impossible to get the attention of the waiters, the revolving lights distorting all movement as he waved his arm in their direction.

In the end, he approached the bar, hanging back from the crowded stools. He kept his eyes open for Callaghan, ready to duck away should the proprietor appear. When he was finally served, he carried his drink to the outskirts of the dancefloor, searching the crowds for known pushers. At the far end of the room, he spotted a prowler. A scrawny youth with a pale and pimply face edged close to a table of girls. The girls whispered to each other. Daly halted a few paces from the youth. Sweat trickled down his face, but he was afraid to brush it away in case it attracted their attention. One of the girls stood up, following the youth to the emergency exit. Daly covered the ground silently, keeping them in sight through the crush of bodies. The girl fumbled in a large white purse, extracting a handful of crumpled notes. Daly was less than four feet away, concentrating hard as the youth placed a hand in the pocket of his coat.

'Sergeant Daly,' Callaghan boomed. 'What a pleasure to see you.'

Daly's heart skipped a beat. He spun round to see the smiling face of Callaghan inches from his own. When he turned back, the girl and the youth had gone.

Garda Macklin put his hand to his head, feeling the cold sweat that had broken on his brow. His partner, O'Brien, held his ground, taking a handkerchief from his pocket and putting it to his mouth.

Stretched out on the grass, like a dissected frog in a laboratory, lay Simon Toman, his lifeless eyes staring out into space. The skin of his face was contorted, the lips drawn back in a snarl, exposing the even white teeth and pale pink gums.

His left arm was thrown back above his head, his hand held in place by a metal spike driven through the palm. The right hand lay loosely at his side, the flesh shredded where, in some dreadful agony, he had ripped it free of impalement.

A pool of blood congealed on the ground where his genitals had been, and a ribbon of red trailed out into the grass, leading from a gaping stomach to a glistening pile of innards.

CHAPTER EIGHT

Dublin, Sunday May 27th

Brendan Rafferty paced the living room leaving a trail of cigarette ash in his wake. Sean Rafferty slept in an armchair, a glass balanced precariously on his knee. Pale morning light filtered into the room through a chink in the curtains and cast a grey graveyard pallor on the scene. Bottles littered the room and here and there a glass lay awry.

An ambulance wailed past in the distance.

With growing agitation Brendan glanced at his watch, then at the telephone. Upstairs the toilet flushed and he wondered whether Rose would come down and make them coffee. He heard the bedroom door click shut and he cursed. *Stupid bloody woman, no bloody use, except for dolling herself up! And Sean, just as useless! Imagine letting a fool like him look after the street end of things!* Unable to stand the silence, he kicked his brother's foot, sending the glass and its contents crashing to the floor. Sean woke with a strangled cry, his arms beating at his sodden trousers.

'You claimed you could look after the pushers,' Brendan sneered. 'Wasn't I a bloody idiot for thinking you could do anything right?'

'What time is it?' asked Sean.

Brendan sat down, glad to take the weight off his feet. They had picked up the rival pusher and driven him out to the Bond Street area of the docks where they had let Charlie soften him up. The results had been disappointing, but they should not have expected more. The boy had known nothing of his supplier other than the fact that he received a telephone call twenty four hours prior to each drop. He met the supplier at a different place each time. A vague description of the man and, of course, no name. With three teeth less than when they had picked him up, they had let the pusher go.

Now one of their own was missing, a pusher who knew where the 'safe' houses were, where the bulk of the drugs were stored. If he talked they would be in trouble. After satisfying themselves that he had not been picked up by the police they had put every available man on the streets, covering pubs, clubs, the discos and the estates. A few reports had trickled in, but all negative.

'Tell Rose to make us some coffee,' Brendan said. He sat by the telephone, his fingers tapping on the table.

'She'll be down in a minute,' Sean said, returning from the hall.

The phone rang and Brendan made a dive for it. He listened intently to the voice at the other end.

Sean watched the colour drain from his brother's face, watched the deliberate way he replaced the receiver. 'What is it?' he asked.

Brendan's voice was a mixture of bewilderment and anger. 'They killed Simon,' he said. 'The rotten bastards killed Simon.'

Superintendent Walsh looked over the bridge he had made with his fingers and raised an eyebrow quizzically.

'We had him in on suspicion once,' Carney said. 'Definitely one of Rafferty's men.' He was still stunned from viewing the Garda photographs.

'Could it be the work of a junkie? Someone desperate for a shot?'

Carney shook his head. 'Not unless they walk around with spikes in their pockets.'

'Any theories?'

'Not at the moment. I thought of the Flanagans, but they couldn't sustain a war with the Raffertys.'

'Sinn Fein?' suggested Walsh. 'They've been muscling in on the tenants associations. Could be this was a warning?'

'Possibly, but a bit over the top. Whoever did this must be psycho.'

'Keep in touch with the Murder Squad,' Walsh told him. 'No point in duplicating the work.'

By the end of the morning Carney had gone through all the files. There was no trace of a lead. He gazed dismally at the top of his desk. Daly appeared at the door. 'Nothing.'

'I think it's time we went out and about,' said Carney.

It took them an hour to locate The Mouse, a freckle-faced youth with a pointed nose and a habit of constantly sniffing. The Mouse settled back in his seat, enjoying the ride. Carney had helped him with his drug problem and he trusted the Inspector enough to pass on pieces of information that he gleaned from the streets.

'I heard about it this morning,' The Mouse said. 'Bad scene. Rafferty had his men out asking questions. No one seems to know anything. Or, if they do, they aren't saying. You can't blame them, not after what happened to Toman.'

'Any strangers pushing at the flats?'

'One guy last week. Claimed he could fix something up. Young lad. About my age. Tall. Didn't seem to know what he was doing.'

'How do you mean?'

'Didn't know the slang words. Wasn't sure of the price . . . or the quality. If you're a pro you know these things.'

'What do you make of it then?'

'Seems to me someone who doesn't know much about the business has got hold of a supply and is trying his luck.'

Carney began to head back into the city. 'You don't just come across a supply of this stuff,' he said. 'To supply at a rate where the competition notice, it has to be a fair amount. That takes planning and a lot of money.'

'Might be coming in from the North. Someone up there trying to get in on the act, recruiting pushers down here. It would be safer to sit up there and let your men on the street take all the flak.'

Carney made a mental note to contact the RUC and the Customs and Excise.

'Keep your eyes peeled for the lad you saw last week. Give me a ring, office or home, day or night,' he said as they dropped The Mouse off.

'What do you think?' Daly asked.

'Can't see anyone up North having the necessary contacts, unless we come back to the terrorist groups. It can't be the IRA. They could never live with it politically.'

'Some maverick outfit?'

'Maybe. You know, if we're smart Rafferty will do the job for us. It appears he hasn't a clue what's going on. He has to find out or else his own credibility goes. Watch him and he might solve our problem.'

'A twenty-four-hour surveillance?' Daly suggested with relish. He knew how touchy the subject of overtime was with his boss.

'Don't push your luck,' Carney said, grinning. 'But I'll see what I can do.'

'Lunch?'

'Yes, okay,' Carney sighed. 'What time would we find Mr Callaghan?'

'He's usually there by four.'

'I'm going to enjoy our little visit,' said Carney.

Jockey was nervous. The newspapers carried the story of the murder, but none of the gory details. He had heard them out on the street, each telling making the mutilations worse than the last. Whichever was true it was bad. He knocked on the door of the house in St Anne's Road, force of habit making him glance over his shoulder. The woman who came to the door looked him up and down, her face expressionless even when he gave the password for the day. Without speaking, she disappeared into the house again, leaving him standing nervously on the doorstep. She returned with the envelope which was addressed and stamped. Jockey took it from her, the door closing in his face before he could speak. He folded it down the middle, first making sure that all the individual packets inside had been shaken down to one end. Placing the envelope in his inside pocket, he hurried to his first drop.

Inside the telephone kiosk, he had a good view of the street. He spotted his contact on the other side of the road and he watched as the boy headed towards him.

The boy was in his teens, tall and thin and wearing a loose-fitting raincoat, the collar turned up about his ears. The face was anxious, the eyes darting from side to side, the shoulders held tense, the body leaning forward poised for flight. Even before he reached the box, he had the money in his hand. Jockey allowed the boy to open the door, his hand reaching out to relieve him of the notes. There was no eye contact as the package changed hands and without a word Jockey slipped past him, brisk strides taking him well away in seconds.

Outside Christchurch Cathedral, a girl in a leather coat with a white fur collar brushed against him, the money and the packet changing hands in the blink of an eye. In the grounds of Trinity College two more contacts were made, leaving him with one more before the evening round. He was five minutes early for his rendezvous at the corner of Fenian Street and Denzille Lane and he paused to light a cigarette and inhale deeply. No one had followed him. Sensing that the afternoon was going to pass without incident he relaxed, enjoying the brief respite.

Jockey had a moderate habit, one which he felt he could control. He knew of others who thought the same and were now hopelessly committed, well down the road to destruction. The biggest perk of pushing the drugs was that you were guaranteed a supply. Payment in kind was the only way to operate. With a regular supply the pressure was off. That way you kept out of sight of the law, increasing the chances of survival. No need to resort to stealing, shoplifting or mugging for your existence. He was so lost in his thoughts that he failed to notice the time slipping away. When he did glance at his watch, nearly fifteen minutes had passed and he had the horrible feeling that his contact was not going to show. Fearful of a journey across town with the stuff still on him, he headed for Upper Merrion Street towards UCD and the flat where Maire lived.

He knocked on her door, listening for footsteps, hoping she would be there alone. She was surprised to see him, hesitating and blocking his path as he made to enter. Pushing past he entered the dingy hall, his nose curling at the musty smell coming from the damp mouldy walls.

The living room was a mess. Plates were stacked high on the table. The left-over food, solidified and turning blue, wafted its odours around the room. The walls were covered with graffiti and the carpet had lost its colour under a barrage of stains.

She led him into one of the bedrooms. There were no beds; instead two mattresses had been thrown up against the wall, the sheets grey and grimy, the once white pillows yellowing from the perspiration marks which fused and overlapped each other. A window at the far end of the room was caked in dirt. He had seen it all before.

Maire said nothing, standing instead with her back against the door, her eyes fixed on the floor.

'I want you to do me a favour,' he said, unbuttoning her blouse.

Carney and Daly took the steps up to the disco two at a time. Maeve opened the door a crack, hesitating and looking back over her shoulder.

Seemingly reluctant, she opened it wider and allowed the two men to enter.

'Is your husband in?' Carney asked, taking off his coat and throwing it unsuccessfully at one of the stools.

Daly moved past Maeve to retrieve the coat, glancing into the kitchen and behind the bar as he did so. He picked up the coat, shaking his head.

'Won't be back till later,' Maeve replied. 'Sorry you missed him.'

'Don't mind if I use your toilet?' Daly asked.

'Why don't you go and piss somewhere else?' she said, heading towards the bar.

'Maeve Callaghan,' Carney scolded. 'And I thought you liked us.'

Daly returned a few seconds later, Callaghan following close behind. 'He was here all the time,' Daly said, in mock surprise. 'Wasn't that fortunate?'

'Come and sit down,' Carney invited, pushing out a stool with his foot. 'It's not very often we get the chance of a cosy chat.'

'I don't have to answer any questions,' Callaghan said, defiantly. 'I told you before, I have nothing to say.'

Carney reached forward, grabbing him by the throat. 'Listen, you slimy piece of shit. You and I are going to have a little talk and you're going to give me some answers.'

Callaghan's eyes opened wide in surprise, his hands flying automatically to grab the wrist at his neck. He felt the edge of a stool being pressed against the back of his knees and his legs buckled.

Carney released his grip, stepping back. He nodded to Daly who positioned himself at Callaghan's shoulder.

'You're in a lot of trouble,' Daly whispered in Callaghan's ear. 'I suggest you think carefully about how you're going to talk yourself out of it.'

Callaghan straightened his crumpled collar and started to massage his neck.

'You can start by telling us what you know about last night,' Carney said, towering over the shaken man.

'What about last night?' Callaghan asked.

Carney picked up a glass from the bar. He held it up to the light, shaking his head.

'Really,' said Callaghan. 'I don't know what it is you want.'

Carney hurled the glass straight-armed down the length of the dancefloor. It shattered on impact. Jumping up on the counter he reached over, removing a bottle of Powers whiskey from its holder.

Maeve appeared from the kitchen, a dishcloth and a dripping plate in her hand.

'What was that?' she asked.

Carney ignored her, testing the weight of the bottle by tossing it from one hand to the other.

Callaghan indicated to his wife that she should stay. 'You crazy bastard,' he spluttered, trying to raise himself from the stool. Daly placed a hand solidly on his shoulder and forced him back into his seat.

'You've got ten seconds,' Carney warned him. 'If you haven't told me something I haven't heard before you won't be having a dance tonight. You'll be too busy picking glass from the floor.'

Maeve threw the dishcloth on the counter. 'You can't do this,' she said, her face reddening.

'Ten, nine, eight . . .' Daly began to count.

'Why don't you ask me the questions?' Callaghan said.

'Well,' said Carney, placing the bottle within easy reach. 'Let's start with Simon Toman.'

'I had nothing to do with that.'

'Believe me,' Carney said, placing a hand on the bottle again, 'if I thought you did we wouldn't be talking together in such a friendly manner. He was here last night?'

Callaghan glanced quickly at his wife. 'I saw him about. He was in and out.'

'Who else did you see?'

Daly stood closer. 'You remember seeing me?'

'Yes. I remember seeing you. So what?'

'Who were you protecting?' Carney asked, picking up the bottle.

'Protecting? I wasn't protecting anyone.'

The bottle spun in a lazy arc, glinting as it tumbled. It landed with a sharp crack, the contents spraying out, fumes filling the air. Carney picked up another bottle and studied the label, beginning to wonder if he had overstretched himself. Not much more to lose, he thought, deciding he would try one last time.

'The word was out,' Callaghan said suddenly. 'The word was out that someone was trying to muscle in.'

'That's better,' Daly said, patting Callaghan on the shoulder.

'Toman picked one of them out. Wanted to have a word with him, that's all.'

'So what happened next?'

'Toman followed his man out. That's all I know.'

'Neither of them came back?'

'Toman came in about an hour later.'

'You talked to him?'

Callaghan again looked at his wife. 'Might have had a quick word. Nothing special.'

'You asked him what happened,' Carney suggested, 'and he told you.'

Callaghan thought long and hard before answering. 'He said they had asked him a few questions.'

'Let's see if I have this right so far,' Carney said. 'Here was someone fouling the patch. Someone else pushing drugs on Brendan Rafferty's territory. Not to worry though, must be some sort of misunderstanding. Nothing that a little chat couldn't put right. So they collar him outside, point out the error of his ways, pat him on the head and send him home to mother. Is that about it?'

Callaghan shrugged.

'No,' said Daly. 'I think you have it all wrong. I think they took the man somewhere quiet, beat his brains in and dumped him. What they didn't know was that the other side had the same idea, only they weren't kidding. They picked Toman up shortly after losing their own man, took him out and castrated him and sent Brendan Rafferty a message without words.'

'It's getting rough out there,' Carney said, shaking his head sadly. 'You never know where it will end. Think of the mayhem you could let loose in a place like this. Toss in a petrol bomb, jam the doors.'

'You're not keeping anything back, are you?' Daly asked.

Callaghan shook his head.

Carney lobbed the bottle six feet into the air, slightly to Callaghan's right. Callaghan was slow to react, his fingers barely touching the spinning object.

'You'll have to be faster on your feet than that,' Carney commented, nodding briefly to Maeve as he turned and left.

CHAPTER NINE

Dublin, Monday May 28th

Pat Hume whistled as he walked towards St Stephen's Green. To date he had been the most successful of the group. He had twelve regular junkies buying from him now, bringing in over sixteen hundred punts a week. The work was easy, the perfect selling job. Customers went to any lengths to seek him out, the deal was in cash, the hours of work short.

For eighteen years all he had known was poverty. Living with an alcoholic mother, not knowing his father who disappeared just after he was born, his life had been a series of hardships. Looking back, he found it hard to remember any good times. The other children called him the Duke of Wellington because his mother could not afford to buy him shoes. They teased him because he had no father. His formal education had ended at the age of thirteen, his mother moving from slum to slum, not bothering to send him to school. Now all that was over. Now he had a cause. The old order in Ireland was to be swept aside. To achieve this, the struggle would be long and hard. Innocent people would be hurt, but the result would justify all of their actions. Crowe had said it would be so.

He turned and walked through the concrete arches of the block of flats, taking a kick at an empty coke can, listening to it rattle into the darkness ahead. Two young boys ran past him, their heads bent, an adult voice crying after them, threatening them with terrible retribution. As he entered the forecourt a man emerged from one of the ground-floor flats, a brush in his hands, his feet crunching over broken glass.

Hume paid scant attention, turning abruptly left, and heading for the stairs. A cat shot by, something furry hanging from its jaws. On the second flight he paused for a rest, his breath coming in short gasps. When he had recovered sufficiently he continued, taking the rest of the steps at a more leisurely pace.

The youth and the girl sat together on the bottom stair of the sixth floor, their arms around each other, their faces pale and shiny, a thin sheen of sweat covering their brows. The girl looked up as he approached, relief showing in her eyes.

Taking the money from the outstretched hand he carried on up the stairs, pausing only when he had turned the corner out of sight. Waiting for a while, he retraced his steps, dropping the packet on their laps as he passed.

Covering the descent at a brisker pace, he stopped once, sure that there were footsteps ahead of him. He peered over the bannisters, unable to see the source of the sound. Continuing cautiously, his ears straining, he finally stepped out into the forecourt. The man with the brush was still there, sweeping glass against the wall.

Mad Johnny paused from his work. He watched as the boy left the flats, marking down in his mind every detail of clothing, every mannerism of his walk, even the tune that he whistled.

Jockey was in his element. The clouds had rolled in over the city, blotting out the moon, turning the streets into an ideal place of refuge. He had taken one less packet on his latest collection, to compensate for the short delivery of the afternoon. The wind blew down the street, chasing debris alongside his feet. He loved the feeling of anonymity, welcoming the darkness that protected him. He avoided the major roads whenever he could, scurrying quickly across them when there was no other way.

Tonight, after his usual round of drops, he had been given a special task, being personally briefed by Sean Rafferty. The task was ideally suited to him. No one had the stealth of foot that he possessed. He was an expert at trailing silently and surely. He knew all the tricks and dodges of the hunted.

Pearse Station was the area he had been assigned and it suited his style well. There were plenty of dark corners in which to hide, many exits to choose from should a quick withdrawal be required. He began by completing a leisurely circuit of the surrounding streets, assessing the pedestrians in the area, moving in eventually to the station precincts, sorting out the genuine travellers from those whose purpose was not connected with trains. For some it was a meeting place, for others a refuge from the elements, but for two or three it was as he suspected.

He decided to take a chance, singling out the most obvious candidate for his attention. The girl was very young, no more than fifteen or sixteen, wearing a pair of tight-fitting jeans, a vivid red sweater and a short denim jacket. Her long, black hair was swept back and tied in a pony tail. A brown bag with a gold clasp swung from her shoulder, dangling at the end of a tarnished chain. She hung back from the open spaces, taking positions against vending machines and buttresses in the wall. To Jockey, the giveaway signs were the nervous glances at her watch, the occasional clutching of her stomach and a growing agitation which had her pacing nervously to and fro as time passed.

Jockey smiled to himself. Always keep them waiting. It was only a matter of time before her pusher showed.

He spotted the boy before she did and turned his back on the scene to view it through the reflection from a glass window. The drop was made casually, the girl jamming the packet into her bag, the pusher moving quickly away from her. Jockey edged along the wall, keeping the boy constantly in his sights. His quarry walked quickly down Westland Row, crossing the road and turning right into Lincoln Place. Jockey followed about fifty yards behind.

Five minutes later the boy stopped outside the Bank of Ireland building at College Green where another drop was made to a contact Jockey recognised. One of the missing users took the packet from the boy, then disappeared quickly in the direction of Trinity College. Now the chase took on a more personal meaning for Jockey. Here was the one who had been causing him so much trouble.

Brendan Rafferty took a handful of ice cubes from the ice bucket and dropped them into his glass. Whiskey splashed over the edge of the glass and ran down the back of his hand. Sean watched him closely, trying to assess his mood. The evening had ended as Sean had known it would, with the hawkish attitude prevailing. More than twenty men were on the streets, searching out the renegade pushers. And when they tracked one down . . .

Rose looked round the door and beckoned to Sean. He joined her. 'What's going on?' she asked.

'Brendan has the pushers out trying to track them down.'

'Is that bad?'

The telephone rang and Sean quickly closed the door on his wife. 'Stay there,' he heard his brother say. Then Brendan slammed the phone down. 'Your friend, Jockey. He followed one of them to Dalkey.'

'Give Charlie and Boyle a ring,' Brendan called to Rose as the two men headed for the door. 'Tell them we'll pick them up.'

They changed cars at Charlie's house. Charlie was a big man, treated by many as stupid. He sat sideways in the back seat, flexing his ham-like fists. Charlie enjoyed using his fists, especially in the service of the Raffertys. They had been good to him. First the father, in the good old days: Old Man Rafferty had appreciated muscle, had treated Charlie properly, at times almost as a member of the family. And now Brendan . . . Brendan had his faults, was always shouting at people, but rarely did he shout at Charlie.

Beside Charlie sat the smaller figure of Tony Boyle. A shock of red hair lay across his forehead and freckles merged into large masses on his pale skin. Boyle was a newcomer to the mob, taken on by Brendan Rafferty when the Flanagans decided he was too dangerous to keep around. Twice he had jeopardised Flanagan operations when his victims had ended up making statements to the Drug Squad from hospital beds. 'They say I'm making a mistake,' Brendan had said when he agreed to recruit him. 'They tell me you'll have Carney and his people sniffing around and finding things to hang on me. Hope you don't prove me wrong, taking you on.'

They met Jockey outside the call box. Jockey pointed out the house and left. They eased the car forward to a spot opposite the front gate. Charlie was despatched to the back of the house to confirm that the occupant was alone. 'Just the one,' he informed them on his return.

‘You and Boyle take the front,’ said Brendan. ‘Sean and I will take the back.’ There were no lights at the rear and the moon appeared only fleetingly. The back of the house was dark and they had to feel their way along the rough brick. As far as the two men could make out there were low steps leading to the back door and an uneven brick path ran down to what seemed to be a greenhouse. They positioned themselves on either side of the door, waiting for Charlie’s knock at the front.

When Pat Hume heard the knocking he immediately assumed that some of the others had returned. It was only when he stepped into the hall that he had second thoughts. There should have been no need to knock. They all had keys. He stopped in his tracks, straining to hear a familiar voice. When he heard none, he doubled back and dodged into the dining room.

Brendan tried the back door, finding it bolted. He edged away, staring at the upstairs bedroom windows. He heard Charlie rattling the front door, then footsteps from somewhere inside. A sound of falling crockery and a muttered curse came from the kitchen. Brendan tensed his muscles and looked at his brother. Sean was breathing heavily, his hands clenched into fists. As the back door burst open they launched themselves at the startled figure, bundling him back into the house.

CHAPTER TEN

Dublin, Wednesday May 30th

It always struck Carney as ironic that Garda Síochána Headquarters should be on the other side of the road from the zoo, and especially appropriate that the Commissioner's offices should have a splendid view of the exhibits. The Administration, the Murder Investigation Squad and the Forensic Science laboratories for the Dublin Garda were all housed within sight and sound of screeching monkeys, lions, tigers, wallabies and secretary birds. The last time the Deputy Commissioner had called a full-scale meeting had been on the black Monday when five cars belonging to patrons of the zoo had been burglarised as they sat beneath the Commissioner's window. Commissioner Davis had found the episode especially galling since the discarded suitcases and handbags had been returned to them by the Army who occupied the McKee Barracks at the back of the station.

When Carney arrived Deputy Commissioner Devlin broke off his conversation with Chief Superintendent Byrne of the Murder Squad. He waved Carney into the office and offered him a chair opposite Superintendent Walsh. Carney took his place, glancing quickly at his colleagues, trying to gauge the nature of the proceedings. His spirits sank as the door was closed, indicating that all the participants were assembled. He would have liked others of his own rank in attendance. He had the unpleasant feeling that any actions originating from their discussions would be delegated downwards, responsibility for translating decisions into practice to rest ultimately with him.

'The Commissioner dined with the Minister last night,' Devlin said.

Carney felt a fluttering in his stomach.

'During this little tête à tête,' Devlin continued, 'the discussion naturally turned to this.'

That morning's edition of the *Irish Times* slid gently over the polished desk, coming to rest with the headline facing Carney.

The *Irish Times*, for all its conservatism, had been unable to refrain from following the lead of the more sensational dailies. It featured a dark and gloomy picture of the inside of a kitchen, a body, covered with a white sheet, lying on the floor. In the background two Garda officers were kneeling, their faces as white as the sheet that claimed their attention. The kitchen walls above the fitted cupboards were streaked with what the reader could only imagine was blood.

The headline read 'SLAUGHTERHOUSE 9', the number taken from the address of the house where the body had been discovered.

Carney reached forward, turning the paper slightly to share the report with Byrne. Byrne's reaction was to ignore it, concentrating his attention instead on a spot above and beyond Devlin's gaze.

'It has to be stopped,' Devlin said. 'It has to be stopped quickly. The reason I've called you in this morning is to find out how best we can achieve a result.' He swivelled his chair to face Walsh. 'What have we got so far?'

Walsh cleared his throat. 'At 10.35 yesterday morning a Mr Robert Whelan, employed by the owners as a window cleaner, was engaged at the premises. He noticed blood on the kitchen walls as he looked through the window. When the officers arrived they searched the premises and discovered approximately seven ounces of heroin taped to the underside of the electric cooker. The body, so far unidentified, was severely mutilated. The details are in the pathologist's report, along with the official photographs. We've questioned all the neighbours. No one heard anything unusual or saw anyone enter or leave the premises. Time of death is estimated at between 12 and 2 a.m. yesterday morning.

'The owners of the property are Cork based. They rent the premises out, using J. F. Falloon and Sons. We contacted the agents and found that the house was rented to a Martin Maguire who gave a London address. We're checking that out now with Scotland Yard.'

'It has striking similarities with the Toman killing,' said Devlin. 'Carney?'

Carney paused before he committed himself. It had taken him years of gentle persuasion to wean his office away from headquarters. The last thing he wanted was some joint investigation with the Murder Squad.

'We know that shortly before his death Toman fingered a rival pusher,' he began, 'although we don't know who, or what the outcome was. Shortly after Toman left the club to follow the pusher he returned and was seen by the club owner, Callaghan. Some time after that Toman was found in the Botanic Gardens. Callaghan is part of, or at least has connections with, the Raffertys. We've picked up pushers from time to time on his premises. We assumed that the Raffertys would react in some way to the Toman killing.'

'You think the Raffertys are responsible for this?'

'No proof, but we're making enquiries.'

'My men are interviewing them,' said Byrne.

Devlin began to tap his heel against the wooden floor. 'I hope we're not duplicating the effort on this. Perhaps we should combine resources for this operation. Gather the squads together and use headquarters as the centre.'

'I don't think we need go that far,' Walsh said quickly, earning Carney's gratitude. 'We'd lose time moving men and files. I think we can work something out between us that will avoid that problem.'

Devlin pushed his chair away from the desk. 'I want a daily report,' he said. 'Byrne, you take responsibility. I want to know the results of both your enquiries. Have it on my desk by six each evening.'

'How would you like a bit of overtime?' Carney asked, beckoning Daly to his office. 'See some night life? Mingle with people your own age?'

'I take it you had an interesting session with the Deputy Commissioner?'

'We had a narrow escape,' said Carney. 'He suggested we move in with Byrne to avoid duplication of effort. Thank God Walsh was there.'

'And all this leaves us . . . where?'

Carney pushed a jotter and pencil across the desk. 'We leave the murder investigation to Byrne, let him worry about the Raffertys. I want you to get in touch with the Special Branch. I want any information on the whereabouts of known terrorists, all the latest gossip. I want the up-to-date situation on the composition of the Provos and INLA. Names, positions in the organisations, especially any information on anyone who might have drifted away recently. When you have that, get hold of Customs and Excise in Belfast. Joe Purnell should be able to help. Ask him if he has any information on major drug movements in Europe, whatever the type or source. Check with Interpol for the latest from their agents. Check with the parole office and see if anyone has broken off with them. Check with the labs for the composition of the heroin found yesterday and ask Interpol if they have a match. After lunch phone Byrne's office and see if Scotland Yard have traced this . . . Martin Maguire, the one who rented the house.'

Daly stood up, still pencilling notes on the pad. 'And phone my wife,' Carney called as Daly disappeared into the corridor, 'and tell her I'll be late. Very late!'

Paris, Wednesday May 30th

Taggart paced the room of the hotel, wearing a path between the bed and the dressing table, his limp becoming more pronounced as the leg stiffened. His hand clenched a piece of lined notepaper that had been delivered ten minutes earlier through the Libyan People's Bureau. The news contained in the note was not good. Two killings in two days, and the Garda crawling all over the place – the last thing he needed. Now they would have to slow down the operation, even suspend it for a time. No, not that! Time was the last thing he could afford to lose. With the European elections a little over two weeks away, they needed the money to pay for the arms or else they would lose the publicity value of the attack. There might not be another media-intensive event for months and he knew he could not keep the tenuous hold he had on his group in Ireland without some immediate action.

No slowing down, no suspension of the operation, not when they were so close. Not when most of the money was already waiting for him in London. Just a little bit more, and the deal could go ahead.

Reading the piece of paper one more time, he set fire to it, watching it curl and blacken in the glass ashtray. Reluctantly he began to pack his suitcase, throwing his clothes in haphazardly. There was nothing more for him to do on the Continent. One stopover in London, then back to Ireland.

After many months, Taggart was going home.

Dublin, Wednesday May 30th

Carney poured himself some soup from the battered blue flask, wiping the sides as the ill-fitting vacuum chamber seeped the thick liquid down the sides. On his desk was a bundle of papers and yellow files, each marked with lettering in broad felt-tipped pen. He took a last look at the lists of Provo and INLA hierarchies, then consigned them to his pending tray. The soup tasted dreadful and he realised it was now nearly twelve hours since he had eaten.

Daly leafed through a stack of notes, trying to locate the page that had the information from Interpol. 'Here it is,' he said, taking out a crumpled sheet. 'Ever heard of a man called Taggart?'

Carney put his cup down and kicked his chair back from the desk so that he could stretch. 'Doesn't ring any bells.'

'The CIA received a request for information from the Kuwaiti Government over a month ago. Apparently a man was stabbed to death in the middle of the city. They caught one of the killers, a Libyan student called Kamel. Claimed he was working for a man called Taggart. The Kuwaitis contacted the States who turned up nothing and passed it on to Interpol. They contacted the Yard.'

'And did the Yard get in touch with us?'

'There's nothing in the records.'

'Sometimes,' said Carney, 'I wonder how we ever survive. Didn't it strike anyone that Taggart was an Irish name? What's the description?'

'There isn't one.'

'You're sure? The Kuwaitis apprehend a man suspected of murder. He tells them he's working for a man called Taggart and they don't give us a description!'

'The telex just gives the bare facts.'

Carney was disgusted. 'Get back to them and ask for a full description. If they can't give you one get in touch with the Foreign Office and ask them to get on to whoever it was in the Kuwaiti Government who started all this. Check if the murder was drug related.'

He reached over, rescuing the papers from his pending tray. 'And while you're at it, get me photographs and descriptions of all the men on this list. If you have any trouble with Special Branch get Walsh to handle it.'

As far as Carney was concerned, the scum of the drug world could do what they wanted to each other; what he feared most was an escalation of the drug supply. He was in enough trouble already.

'I'm going out,' he called to Daly as he walked towards the reception area. 'I'll be back in an hour.'

CHAPTER ELEVEN

Dublin, Thursday May 31st

The girl slipped out of the flat, closing the door gently, frightened that she would disturb her mother who was snoring loudly on the couch. The corridor was quiet, except for the distant sounds of a baby crying. Siobhan Lennon breathed a sigh of relief. Listening at the door for a few seconds, she could hear her heart thumping against the thin cotton of her blouse.

She had almost not survived. The days since her mother had found her on the stairs had been long and agonising. Locked in her room, with no way of reaching her pusher, she had endured the withdrawal symptoms alone, her stomach heaving, her body shaking the bed so much that her mother had strapped her down with strips of old sheets. She had writhed about in a twilight world, wallowing in her own vomit.

Now, with the worst over, she had convinced her mother to let her up. It had surprised her how calm she had been that morning, washing and dressing, eating the enormous breakfast that had been laid before her, all the time her body screaming for a fix, her nerve ends jangling. Yet she had suppressed it all, smiling at the conversation, volunteering to wash the dishes. It had worked. Not only had her mother left her alone in the house, she had resumed her lunchtime drinking which meant she would sleep for most of the afternoon.

That was all the time Siobhan needed to contact her man.

Descending the steps two at a time, she covered the three flights quickly. Ignoring the call box opposite the flats, she dodged the traffic on the road, heading for the bar at the corner of the intersection.

The lounge was fairly quiet and no one paid any attention to her as she fumbled with the coins in the slot. To her relief, the ringing tone purred comfortingly at the other end. After thirty seconds her heart began to sink.

Leaving the bar, she headed back to the flats, bounding up the stairs despite the pain in her side and the gnawing feeling in her stomach. On the second floor she knocked urgently on a door. Inside, she heard a shuffling sound and the noise of a lock being turned. Tommy peered out at her, his face white and waxy.

'Tommy?' she said, alarmed at his appearance. 'Are you okay?'

Tommy opened the door wide, allowing her to squeeze past him. 'Have you seen him?' Tommy asked, his voice trembling.

'Seen him?' Siobhan repeated numbly. 'I thought . . .'

'He didn't come round. Hasn't been for two days.'

'Where have you been getting your fix?' Siobhan asked. She knew the answer before he spoke. His eyes were glazed, a film of sweat covered every portion of exposed flesh and his arm was constantly being wiped across his nose, the sniffling sounds muffled against his sleeve.

She sank into a threadbare wing chair and tried desperately to concentrate. She knew of one other contact, her original supplier, but that would mean a trek through the city.

'Have you any change?' she asked him, shaking him by the shoulder when he did not answer. 'Change, Tommy, for the bus.'

The boy fumbled in his pockets producing two coins which he held out in a shaky hand.

'Give me your money too,' Siobhan said. 'I'll get some for you as well.'

An hour later, mingling with the crowds returning to their offices, she waited outside the Dental Hospital in Lincoln Place, searching the corner of Westland Row which led down to the station.

Carney knew from the excitement in Daly's eyes that he had dug up something of interest.

'The murder in Kuwait *was* drug connected,' said Daly. 'Kamel told the authorities that the man they murdered was a supplier and that they had decided to take action against him to protect the population.'

'Where does Taggart fit in?'

'Kamel claimed that Taggart financed the job.'

'Sounds crazy. What sort of set up was it supposed to be? A group of Libyan students and possibly an Irishman in some sort of philanthropic conspiracy to protect the population of Kuwait. I've seen better plots in Starsky and Hutch.'

'The plot thickens,' Daly informed him. 'Kamel didn't last very long in jail. They found him hanged in his cell, three days after they picked him up.'

'What about the description?'

'Kamel claimed he only met him once. Small, five foot five to five foot six, dark hair, balding and walked with a limp.'

'Did you get the photographs and descriptions from Special Branch?'

'Walsh is bringing them over this afternoon.'

'Well,' said Carney, rubbing his hands together. 'Could be very interesting. Anything else?'

'Not so far. I'm waiting for Joe Purnell to call back. Their latest tip-off was about a consignment of cannabis. No heroin problems. He's put the word out to his agents and will get back to us.'

'I think it's time we paid a visit to some of our ex-customers,' Carney said, jumping up from his chair. 'Get your coat.'

Jockey held the girl against the wall, his arm pressurising her throat.

'He came to the flats,' Siobhan sobbed, her breath coming in gasps. 'It saved me coming all this way.'

Jockey eased the arm away, swivelling his head from side to side, glancing up and down the street. 'You'll have to wait,' he hissed in her ear. 'I only carry enough for the drops.'

'When should I meet you?' Siobhan asked, her lips quivering, her tongue pressed hard against the roof of her mouth to choke back the tears.

Jockey let go, taking a step back. He would have to check with Rafferty to see who was covering the flats. He had an inkling it must be Toman and Toman was dead, hence the explanation of no Rafferty contact for the girl. It might just be that the pusher who had muscled in was also dead. The very one Jockey had followed.

'I'll come to the flats later today.'

'I live on the third floor. I usually wait on the stairs of the sixth floor.'

'Okay,' Jockey said. 'I'll meet you there between five and six.'

'There's Tommy,' Siobhan said. 'I'll need one for him.'

Jockey grabbed her by the collar. 'Make sure no one else is with you. Is that clear?'

'You will bring two?' she called after him.

Jockey picked up the phone in the station call box. 'I need to talk to you,' he said when the phone was answered. He replaced the telephone and waited. It usually took Sean Rafferty five or six minutes to leave the house to get to a safe box. Jockey lounged against the door, pretending to count the change in his pocket, but the station was almost empty and no one bothered him. When the call was returned he snatched it from the cradle immediately. 'I think we have some lost sheep coming back to the fold. Did Toman cover St Mary's flats?'

'I think so,' replied the voice on the other end.

'I think our friend had moved in there as well. No one seems to be supplying the area. Any objections if I go in tonight?'

There was a pause. 'No, I suppose not, but be careful. When you make the drop sniff around and see what you can find out. Don't call the house again until I give you the all-clear. The pigs are watching us day and night. The phone might be tapped. Ring Callaghan with any messages. Go and see him anyway. Toman was using his place as well and we need someone to fill in temporarily.'

The phone went dead. The more business Jockey handled the larger his cut and the larger the supply of dope for himself. With the girl Maire beginning to perform for his friends, he was building up a nice little nest egg of his own.

Siobhan put her arm round Tommy. She had known him all her life. They had played together in each other's apartments for as long as she could remember, starting school on the same day, sitting next to each other in class. The relationship had always been an easy one. They could talk to each other without any strain.

Tommy was one month older, his freckly face and ginger hair making him seem younger than he was. It was Siobhan who had carried the relationship into the adult world. With her make-up and her high heels, she looked mature and was always the one to buy the tickets for the restricted films, always the one to lead the way into the discos and pubs. She had often wondered whether she was in love with him, but as she could never decide what that meant exactly, she imagined they were simply inseparable friends. It was probably the absence of sex that made their relationship so easy to maintain. She had always felt responsible for him, even more so now. It was she who had bought the first fix and shared it with him. It was all her fault.

'Only a few more hours,' she crooned in his ear, rocking him gently to and fro, fighting all the time to maintain her own grip on reality. They had to last out. Just a few more hours, she repeated to herself, trying to pretend that the time would fly.

Carney cruised along the pavement, one hand on the wheel, the other tapping out a tune on the dashboard. 'How many times did we collar Toman?' he asked Daly who was munching a sandwich.

Daly swallowed. 'Twice. Once at the disco and once here at the flats. A fine for the first offence, didn't bring him to trial on the second. Trouble with the circumstances of his arrest.'

'Won't be troubling us any more,' Carney said, almost to himself.

'What do you expect to find here?' Daly questioned.

Carney noticed the scepticism in the voice. 'Rafferty loses a pusher. What does he do? He fills the gap. Ask a few questions, see what's new.'

He parked the car, winding up the window. 'Let's have a walk round. I could do with some fresh air.'

Jockey slipped out of the side street, surveying the stark outline of the flats against the pale blue sky. A flock of pigeons wheeled in perfect formation, swooping and diving in the still air. A large, black dog barked at the shadows, breaking off from time to time to chase its tail. Jockey dug his hands deep into his pockets and crossed the road, skipping over the pavement and slowing only when he was within the shelter of the forecourt. The air was much cooler here, the sun's rays unable to penetrate the maze of walls and staircases. There was little activity. Two stained-faced children kicked an empty cigarette packet to each other, the faded gold box skimming effortlessly on the smooth slabs. Taking a final look into the street, Jockey headed for the stone steps.

On the fifth floor, three men leaned against the wall, smoking and blowing the inhaled air through the bars of the bannisters. They seemed bored, as if tired of waiting. When they heard the footsteps approaching from below, they straightened and stubbed out their cigarettes.

The girl hardly gave them a second glance. She was too busy concentrating her strength on the task of climbing the stairs. Saying a muttered prayer that the man would be on time, she passed the three men quickly. After a few seconds, Mad Johnny appeared. When he saw the men he nodded in the direction of the girl, indicating that she was the one. The three men acknowledged the signal and Mad Johnny turned nervously, his arm feeling for support.

Jockey punched the button on the lift for the fifth time, cursing when the operating light failed to show. It would be a long hard climb. He took the steps two and three at a time until his energy waned, leaving him puffing and panting on the landing.

The three men heard him coming and began to move upwards. They passed the girl sitting on the bottom step of the sixth flight and climbed onto the next flight, stopping just out of sight.

Jockey was enjoying thinking of ways he could get back at the girl for all his trouble. He was about to take another rest when he saw her shoes through the gap in the railings. The girl jumped to her feet, relief spreading over her pale features.

Jockey pushed her back, making her sit, relishing the hard thud and her squeal of pain. He tried to speak but his breathing was too ragged and he stood, his head bent, his chest heaving. The girl reached into her coat to extract the money, offering it to him with trembling fingers. As Jockey reached out to accept he caught sight of a movement from above, a flash of shoes on the stairs.

Siobhan heard the clatter of feet and saw that he was about to bolt. She threw her arms around his legs, bringing him down on the landing, shouts and curses echoing off the walls. Knowing she had less than seconds, she pressed with all her weight on the body wriggling beneath her, her hands frantically searching the pockets of the struggling man. Other hands grabbed at him, wrenching him sideways and away from her. Jockey was shouting, his feet kicking at the doors as he was dragged away. Siobhan held onto his lapels, her knees scraping the concrete as she was hauled with him. As the writhing group started to tumble, she closed her hands over a sleek wad in his back pocket, yanking with all her might as the body began to slip out of her grasp.

The shouting diminished as Jockey was kicked and pushed down the stairs. Siobhan was left, exhausted and gasping, her back resting against the hard wall. Through her tears she started to smile. In her hand, the cellophane packets shining dully in the dim light, was enough heroin to keep Tommy and herself for a week.

Carney took hold of Daly's arm, his ears straining.

'Sounds like a bull elephant,' Daly said, backing in against the wall at Carney's signal.

Carney caught a glimpse of a fair-haired youth in a denim jacket hopping backwards down the strairs, his foot swinging and connecting with something out of sight. A body came tumbling down, two other youths following, kicking and pushing it with their heavy shoes to keep the momentum going. The body lay still, doubled up, blood seeping between the fingers that covered the face.

Carney covered the distance in four strides, his arm reaching out and grabbing the fair-haired youth around the throat. Using his knee as a lever, he propelled the youth backwards with as much force as he could muster, sending him sprawling. Jockey scrambled to his feet, blood pouring from his nose. He staggered over to the wall, glancing first at Carney, then at his assailants.

'Okay,' Carney said, 'we're –'

He stopped in mid sentence, catching sight of Daly's stricken face. Spinning round, he found himself staring into the barrel of a gun. Carney froze, his eyes fixed on the muzzle. It was a six-shot .442-calibre revolver with a two-and-a-half-inch barrel, the type used by the old Royal Irish Constabulary. The paint was stripped from the metal, exposing the dull greyish silver beneath. The hand that held it was steady and the face of the youth was calm and purposeful.

'Over to the wall,' the youth demanded, waving the gun a fraction in the direction of Jockey.

Carney obeyed, walking slowly, never taking his eyes off the youth. He felt a bump in his back as Daly was pushed over to join him.

'Stay exactly where you are,' the youth with the gun said, indicating with his free hand for the others to leave. They acted immediately, running out into the street, one of them raising his arm, signalling to an unseen car. The car reversed into sight, the driver leaning back to open the door.

The youth with the gun regarded Carney coldly. Walking up to Jockey, he lowered the gun. 'Stay away from the flats,' he said matter-of-factly, squeezing the trigger at the same time.

The report reverberated through the flats. The bullet entered Jockey's leg, smashing the shin bone an inch below his kneecap, scattering flesh and bone down the wall.

'Next time,' the youth said, turning to Carney, 'I'll save one for you.'

As the youth retreated towards the car, Carney bent down. 'Give me something to tie on his leg,' he said, holding his hand out to Daly.

The car accelerated away, tyres screeching.

Daly tore feverishly at a white handkerchief, his frustration showing as it refused to rip. Doors banged in all levels of the building, faces peered over bannisters, heads poked suspiciously round corners.

'Someone get me a towel,' Carney shouted, his thumbs pressing down onto the artery in the thigh.

Jockey was in shock. His face was a ghostly white and his limbs were twitching spasmodically.

'Use the car radio,' Carney shouted to Daly. 'Call an ambulance.'

'I called for an ambulance, mister.'

Carney glanced up to see Mad Johnny, his face a mixture of fear and confusion.

CHAPTER TWELVE

Dublin, Friday June 1st

Carney cleared the unsorted accumulation of papers and files from his desk, giving Daly space to spread out the sheets containing photographs and descriptions of known Provisionals and INLA men. Both men studied each picture. They scrutinised hairlines and hairstyles, heights, weights and complexions, and checked them off against descriptions on a separate report. Each time they found one that matched the Kuwaiti information they extracted the sheet, isolating it from the others. When all had been examined they began again, to ensure that none had been missed.

'Seven,' Carney said. 'Give me descriptions for these.' He read each file carefully, tossing rejected ones aside. 'Three possibilities. Christ! Not one of them with a limp!'

'Well, it was a good idea. Perhaps this man Kamel was talking a load of shit. His whole story is crazy.'

'Too much of a coincidence. Rival pushers on the streets, a war practically breaking out, then this request from Kuwait involving drugs, Libyan students and someone with a name that sounds Irish.'

'It needn't be a terrorist connection. Might be straight business.'

Carney shook his head. 'Doubt it, not with the Libyans involved. After the London trouble Gadhafi made it clear he would assist terrorists in Ireland. We know the IRA don't peddle drugs. They couldn't live with it politically, and Sinn Fein have been infiltrating tenants associations to try and stamp out drug trafficking. The attack yesterday was probably a result of their efforts. Somebody picked out a pusher for them. So . . . if not the Provos or INLA, then maybe some maverick outfit.'

'You don't go along with Byrne's idea that yesterday was just another phase in the gang war?'

'Not a chance! Kneecapping is a warning. If the Rafferty clan and their sort had been involved, the victim would be dead. The time for warnings is over.'

'That's it then.' Daly gathered photographs and reports together and started to return them to their envelopes.

'Hell!' Carney exclaimed. 'Leave those there. Get onto Special Branch again. This time find out if any of those we picked out has been involved in any shooting incidents, either here or in the North, since these reports were compiled.' When he saw Daly's puzzled expression he exclaimed. 'The limp, Daly. If it was fairly recent it may not be in the files.'

Saturday June 2nd

Eighteen hours after Daly's request for information a document was delivered by Special Branch courier. Carney had just settled down to a late breakfast of ham sandwich and coffee. The coffee grew cold as he studied the document. When Daly arrived at the station he discovered his Inspector sprawled back in his chair, staring thoughtfully at the ceiling.

Daly picked up the half-eaten sandwich. 'Food for thought?'

Carney roused himself. 'Something like that.' He handed the Special Branch report to Daly. 'According to that, one of our men is in Cork, has been there for several months. They don't know the whereabouts of the other two. Sergeant, how much time did we spend yesterday studying the files?'

'An hour,' said Daly, 'maybe a bit more.'

'Yeah! We looked at the photos and we looked at the histories and we didn't bother to look at the names. One of the three we picked out, one that our friends in Special Branch have no recent information on, is Michael Crowe.'

Daly drew in his breath. 'I'd bet they'd like to know where that lunatic is.' Then he smiled guiltily. 'Sorry about that. Crowe, M. It was one of the names I phoned through.'

'So we're both fools,' said Carney. 'Only problem is, the updated information still doesn't mention a limp, for any of the three.'

'Dead end?'

'Maybe not.' Carney reached out and took the document from Daly. 'Listen to this. On the twelfth of December last a patrol of RUC officers was ambushed near the border at Crossmaglen. A number of shots was fired at their car, killing one officer and wounding another. The British Army had a helicopter in the vicinity and it spotted the men running across open fields towards the border. They managed to fire off some shots and they claimed one of the men was hit just as he made it into some woods. A unit of the Irish Army arrived about ten minutes later and found nothing.'

'You think it might have been Crowe?'

'Obviously the Special Branch think so,' said Carney, 'or they wouldn't have bothered to include the incident here. The interesting thing is that neither the Provos nor INLA claimed responsibility and, knowing how efficient they are at getting their claims to the media, it's a fair indication that neither group had anything to do with it. And if it wasn't the Provos or INLA, then who? Some third force? Crowe was disowned by the Provos a long time ago. Politically indefensible.'

'I thought he went over to INLA?'

'The word is they kicked him out after the North Down killings.'

'And he continued the fight on his own?'

Carney considered the situation for a moment. 'They never traced Crowe after North Down. He just vanished. What if he were the man shot in the woods? What if they shipped him out of the country for treatment and told him not to come back? What if he said *sod it* and decided to strike out on his own?'

'Too many *what ifs.*'

Carney smiled. 'I know, but what if I'm right. Get back to Special Branch and ask them for a list of all Crowe's known associates, past and present.'

'But we'll have their names on the other sheets.' Daly was not anxious to bother Special Branch again.

'We'll have all his fighting and political colleagues. We won't necessarily have his friends, those he used during his escapes.'

'No, I suppose not,' Daly agreed reluctantly. 'Do I tell Special

Branch precisely what we're working on, what we want the information for?'

'Tell them what?' asked Carney. 'Tell them that Inspector Carney of the Drug Squad has this hunch about a third terrorist force financing their operation from the proceeds of a drug racket? I don't think so. What we are going to do is get in touch with the police forces of France, Belgium, Germany, Spain and Holland and get them to check their hotel cards for the past month and let us know if they have a Crowe or a Taggart on their lists.'

Daly could see his weekend disappearing beneath a mass of paperwork. 'That will take weeks,' he protested.

'It's all computerised,' Carney said, not really sure if that were true. 'And anyway, what do you think records are kept for in the first place?'

'When will you be back?' Daly asked, as Carney stood up and began to struggle into his coat.

'Not till Monday,' replied Carney cheerfully. 'No need to panic yet.'

London, Saturday June 2nd

The taxi pulled up at the kerb outside the Mayfair Hotel and a uniformed commissionaire stepped forward to open the cab door. The man who emerged allowed his bags to be taken in exchange for a luggage ticket and he made his way to reception, dodging the crowds of tourists and businessmen who thronged the foyer.

He accepted a room in the old wing where the tariff was cheaper, checking in under the name of Rodgers, the name in his present passport. The hotel had been taken over by the Intercontinental chain and was still being refurbished. Upstairs, the corridors were littered with ladders and cans of paint.

The room overlooked the rear entrance of the shops and offices fronting Berkeley Square. Large-diameter pipes, the legacy of Victorian plumbing, ran the length of the skirting board and above the bed was a row of brass buttons that had once been connected with the kitchen.

The man who called himself Rodgers took his cases and tipped the porter. When he had washed and shaved he picked up the phone and dialled a local number.

'Comecon Trade Commission.' The girl's voice was accompanied by clicking and whirring noises from recording equipment.

'Mr Hudek, please.'

'Who is calling?'

'My name is Taggart.'

The line went dead for a moment. Then a male voice spoke. 'Mr Taggart?'

'Is that Joseph Hudek?'

'Yes. It is good to hear from you. Where are you?'

'In London. When can we meet?'

'You want to do business?' Hudek hesitated a moment. Then he said, 'How about tomorrow evening? We could have dinner together? Or would you prefer tonight?'

'Tomorrow's fine. Where?'

'The *Antiquarian,*' said Hudek. 'In Knightsbridge. Shall we say eight o'clock?'

'Eight o'clock.'

Taggart replaced the receiver and smiled. Another day to kill, like the two days he had had to kill in Paris while he waited for the Rodgers passport. Still, this further delay suited him. He had other arrangements to make, and the balance of the cash had yet to arrive.

By Thursday though . . .

They had converted the last delivery into cash almost overnight. Behan had laughed about it when he phoned, laughed about how easy it had been, how the group had practically wholesaled the stuff, how some of Rafferty's men had been buying from them. 'A few more days,' Behan had said, 'and not only will we be rid of every last ounce of it, but you'll have the money, converted into the currencies you've asked for, in your hands in London.'

Taggart sat on the edge of the bed and opened one of the cases. Taking out the large manilla envelopes, he began to count the money that would buy him a place in Irish history.

CHAPTER THIRTEEN

Dublin, Sunday June 3rd

Sinead Carney winced as the sound of the uileann pipes drifted down from her father's bedroom. The dog prowled about the hall, growling softly, its head inclined towards the source of the sound, the hairs on its back beginning to rise. Sinead eased her feet into slippers and padded over to the door.

'Daddy,' she called up the stairs, 'you're driving the dog crazy.'

'Stop teasing them,' Mary called from the bathroom.

'I could have been a musician,' he shouted back. 'I could have been famous.' He climbed on a chair, lifting the pipes to their resting place in a high cupboard. 'You used to like it when my father played them.'

'Your father had a sense of time and place. I never heard him play them at nine o'clock on a Sunday morning.'

'It's the only time I have.'

'That incident the other day isn't bothering you, is it?' Mary asked, joining him in the bedroom.

'No,' Carney assured her. 'They weren't shooting at me.'

'Did you see a doctor?'

'What on earth for?'

'I don't know. Delayed shock. Don't they ask you if you're all right?'

Carney contemplated his wife's question. He had never thought of it before. No one ever asked if you were okay if you were still standing.

'What have you planned for today?' he asked, changing the subject.

'I said I'd go over to my mother's. I don't suppose you want to come.'

'I think I'll cut the hedge,' Carney said, opting for the lesser of two evils.

'On a Sunday?'

'What other day is there?'

Mary plugged in the hair dryer, effectively ending the conversation, the whirring motor drowning the strained silence.

Carney paused at the top of the stairs, allowing Sinead to ease her way past. In a few years the children would be away. They would have lives of their own to lead. Yet he felt as though he hardly knew them. His daughter was at the age when she was filling out, a whole new episode in her life about to unfold. His son seldom spoke to him, even when they were alone in each other's company, which was rarely. Putting the depressing thoughts to the back of his mind he wandered into the garden, dismayed when he saw the height of the grass.

The blades made hard work of the lawn, snagging and sticking from time to time, indifferent to Carney's cursing. He watched his wife and children leave on the way to Mass, none of them turning to wave.

Disowned, he thought grimly.

When they returned he was half way down the hedge, the privets littering the pavement. Mary appeared with a brush and shovel, sweeping the debris away as he cut.

'Did you tell them about your vacation?' she asked.

'Not yet,' he replied. 'I forgot all about it. Doesn't matter when I tell them.'

'Won't they have to make arrangements to cover for you?'

Carney moved to his right and snipped at a protruding leaf. 'I'm the boss,' he replied. 'I make the arrangements.'

'Only eight weeks,' she said, with a shiver of anticipation. 'Eight short weeks and we'll be lying in the sun, long drinks in our hands, nothing to worry about but us.'

For Carney, eight weeks seemed like a lifetime.

Maire Brady slept fitfully, waking every few minutes with the worry of the news from hospital. A friend of Jockey's had passed the word to her, telling her to stay put.

In her handbag, she had enough heroin for one more fix. Sometime in the evening, the man who smelled of fish would be coming to act out his fantasies on her. That would buy two more packets. After that, she had no idea what would happen. It crossed her mind that this might be the time to make a break. Between bouts of light sleep, she lay awake thinking of her family in London. The relationship with her parents was uneasy and it would be difficult to join them. She would have to think of an excuse for dropping out of university, for leaving Dublin.

As the time for her next fix approached, she knew she could never summon the strength to break her habit and face the family. The cramps in her stomach came suddenly. Fumbling for the light switch, she gathered the powder and the syringe from the bedside drawer and made her way to the kitchen. She filled an eyedrop with water and mixed it with heroin in a spoon. Her hands shook as she struck the match to heat the solution.

Lifting her skirt, she stroked the inside of her thigh, coaxing the blue vein to the surface. A drop of blood trickled down her leg when she removed the needle and she dabbed it clean with a dishcloth. By tomorrow afternoon she would be desperate. There was no other way but to go to the hospital and see Jockey. The hopelessness of the situation dissolved as the heroin entered her bloodstream. For a few moments all the troubles of her world disappeared. Closing her eyes she lay back to enjoy what little time was left.

London, Sunday June 3rd

Hudek walked to the restaurant from the main road, his driver following at a discreet distance. In the back of the car, a bodyguard scanned the street, his hand clasped firmly around the butt of a Luger pistol.

At fifty-five, Hudek was being groomed for greater things. On the surface he was an accredited member of the Trade Commission for Communist Economies, fulfilling this role by attending official functions. In practice he worked for an intelligence branch of the Warsaw Pact. He liked his London posting. It was a change from the three dreary years spent in Sofia, a city he hated with a passion. In the relaxed atmosphere of the English countryside he felt at home, his excursions to Cheltenham and Bath reminding him of the cobbled streets and wood-beamed houses of his own city of Prague.

Pulling up the collar of his overcoat, he stepped into the doorway of a shop to strike a match. Lighting a cigarette, he blew a cloud of blue smoke high into the air and watched it fan out on the breeze.

At eight o'clock the limping figure alighted from a taxi. Hudek waited until the man had crossed the road, then stepped from the doorway to follow him. The man sensed movement behind him and stopped.

'Mr Taggart,' said Hudek, 'a pleasure to meet you.'

Inside the restaurant they left their coats with the girl at the desk. The head waiter smiled broadly when he welcomed them. 'Mr Hudek, a delight to see you again . . . and you are very welcome, sir. I have your table ready.'

They ordered drinks at the table and the Irishman surprised Hudek by bluntly asking if everything was ready. 'You are not a businessman, Mr Taggart,' said Hudek. 'Much too forthright. You must learn the subtleties of negotiation.'

'As far as I'm concerned, the negotiations are over. This is simply a question of payment. I believe that in financial circles you come straight to the point.'

Hudek laughed, his pale blue eyes twinkling. 'Quite so.' He raised his glass. 'To the beautiful country of Ireland.'

'To freedom.'

'What are your plans?' asked Hudek and, when Taggart turned to stare at him with suspicion, added, 'Your plans regarding collection?'

'The cargo is at the docks?'

'Ready and waiting.'

'And you have arranged transfer?'

Hudek motioned the waiter over and ordered another drink. 'The captain is waiting only for the time and the place. When you let me know it is as good as done.'

'Thursday afternoon.'

'Ah, I see . . . you have a deadline to meet?'

Taggart ignored the question. He leaned back to allow the

waiter to serve the drinks. Hudek asked for the menu and they ordered their meals. They spoke little during the meal. Hudek watched the other man picking over his steak, obviously without much appetite.

They took their coffee in the lounge where it was cooler. 'You have the money?' Hudek asked.

'Thursday.'

'Good. You pay half to me Thursday before you sail, the other half to the captain when the transfer is complete.'

Taggart shook his head. 'Half to the captain on transfer and the other half when I'm safely in Ireland.'

Hudek pursed his lips. 'How do I know you will pay?'

'How do I know your captain won't dump me overboard?'

Hudek smiled. 'I see the negotiations aren't quite over, Mr Taggart. What do you suggest?'

'There is a man in Brixton,' said Taggart. 'He has a key to a safety deposit box at Euston Station. When I get back safely, I'll telephone him. He will give you the key.'

'I would feel better with a little collateral.'

Taggart fished a pen from his inside pocket and scribbled on a napkin. 'This is his name and address.'

'One of your men?' asked Hudek. 'I have time to check him out.'

Taggart nodded.

They walked together to the end of the street and Hudek saw the Irishman into a taxi. A black limousine drew up as the taxi departed. Hudek climbed into the front seat next to the driver.

'How did it go?' asked a voice from the back.

'No problem,' said Hudek.

CHAPTER FOURTEEN

Dublin, Tuesday June 5th

Carney reached to the back of the telex machine to retrieve the roll of paper that had spilled to the floor. Feeding the stream of paper into the metal retaining clips, he read the messages, stopping half way down when a reference to Paris caught his eye. Ripping the roll in half he tore off the telex from the French police, calling to Daly before he even turned the corner to his office.

Daly was still in his raincoat, tucking his wrapped lunch away in a filing cabinet.

'Taggart!' announced Carney. 'Stayed in the Hotel Montmartre, checked out on Saturday morning.'

'Might be a hundred Taggarts on the Continent at this time of year,' said Daly.

'You've no imagination,' said Carney. 'Get in touch with Aer Lingus and British Airways, check their manifests to see if they have a Taggart on any flight to Dublin. Check all the flights that left Paris in the last three days to whatever destination.'

Daly groaned.

'I'll check the ferry operators,' said Carney, reaching for the telephone directory.

Three hours later the two men sat silent in the office, the desk littered with crumbs and crumpled sheets of notepaper.

'Perhaps he just changed hotels,' Daly suggested.

Carney drummed his fingers on the desk. 'What he did, the miserable bastard, was change names. I know it. Circulate his photograph to all the immigration officials on duty over the weekend and to those on duty today. Put out an alert for him.'

'And the Murder Squad?'

'Everybody,' Carney said. 'Tell them we think Michael Crowe is back in town.'

Walsh was not convinced. 'You don't have any hard evidence that it is Crowe.'

'He's one of a few possibles,' said Carney, 'the most likely of them. And . . .'

'And you've got a feeling. It's one hell of a long shot. There'll probably be a full alert. I just hope we don't finish up with egg on our faces.'

'We've had all the reports except those from Spain. Eight Taggarts so far, but the Paris Taggart is the only one we can't account for at the moment. All the rest are still in their hotels and don't match the description.'

'If he ever did leave Kuwait he could be anywhere by now, most probably in Libya if this Kamel was telling the truth. What makes you think he came to Europe?'

'I don't know where he went, but we have to start somewhere. If this lead comes to a dead end we'll have to broaden the net a bit.'

'If this lead comes to a dead end,' Walsh warned, 'there won't be a net broad enough to catch us.'

'Maybe,' said Carney. He stood up and turned to go, then hesitated. 'Just one thing. If it turns out that Taggart is Crowe and he is in the country, I'd like to be involved in the search.'

'Out of the question,' Walsh said, frowning. 'Special Branch will take over. Christ, if they catch him he probably won't have time for a piss before they extradite him to the North.'

'We have to know what sort of set up he has for the drug traffic . . .'

'Drug traffic? Listen, if what you say is true, then the drugs are a means to an end. When he has what he wants he'll leave the city to the Raffertys again. They're the ones you want to concentrate on.' He joined Carney at the door. 'Anyway, it won't come to that. Taggart will turn out not to be Crowe, and he won't come within a million miles of us. Then, with this alert you're putting out and, God help me, I'm agreeing to, you'll have other things to worry about.'

Maire Brady opened her eyes, to be confronted with the hairy chest of a man she could not recognise. He lay facing her, his head half obscured by the pillow, a low snort coming from his lips as he breathed heavily. Carefully manoeuvering herself to the edge of the bed so as not to disturb him, she closed her eyes and tried to concentrate on the events of the previous night.

She remembered taking fright at the hospital when they began asking her questions about her relationship with Jockey and remembered running out when she was told to report to the policeman in the corridor before going into Jockey's room. From then on her memories were vague. There were flashing lights and a tremendous noise. She had a recollection of a crowd of people and of drinking heavily. She could only assume that she had gone to Callaghan's Disco when the cramps had begun to take hold, although she could not recall how she got there or what had happened. Rolling onto her back, she cleared her mind. Firstly, she felt reasonably calm, which meant she must have managed to score sometime during the night. Immediately this thought struck her she reached out, feeling into the pockets of her skirt which lay by the side of the bed. The slippery surface of the cellophane sent a wave of relief over her and she closed her hands around the packets, drawing her hand to her face to view her prize. Two small cachets of white powder glistened in the light, enough to keep her going for a day and a night.

She suddenly remembered sitting at a bar, watching a whirl of bodies dancing to a cacophonous din, blue and yellow strobe lights twirling about them, making their actions jerky and unreal.

Turning her head to look again at the man beside her, it came back to her. She had accepted his offer of a drink and resisted all his attempts to get her to dance. They had drunk until the bar closed, leaving together and mingling with the crowds on the streets outside. From there she had taken him to the station where they had eventually made a contact, the man financing her purchase. After that her memory began to falter. She was at least thankful she remembered nothing after they arrived at the flat.

She was wondering whether she should try to con him into believing she still had to be paid, when she felt his hand on her thigh and sensed him raising himself from the bed.

Dublin, Wednesday June 6th

Carney ran up the steps to the hospital, avoiding the reception area. He took the stairs instead of the lift to the third floor. The officer on duty stood up briskly when Carney turned into the corridor.

'Any visitors?' Carney asked.

'No, sir. None at all.'

'Good morning,' he called, as he entered the room.

Jockey grimaced. 'I don't have to talk to you.'

'There's gratitude for you. I thought you'd be glad of the company.'

'What do you want?'

'I want to know who those people were and why they wanted to shoot you.'

Jockey closed his eyes. 'How should I know?'

'Seems odd that a gang of youths, fortuitously armed, should suddenly jump out of the shadows and decide to cripple you for life. There must have been a good reason.'

'It must have been a mistake. I'd never been to the flats before.'

'I don't think you had. You know what happened? You were there to take over from your mate, Toman. Unfortunately for you, someone had fingered Toman for them and you got it in his place.'

'I don't know Toman.'

'I suppose you don't know Rafferty either.'

'Right first time.'

'You're in big trouble. What do you think will happen to you now? You'll be laid up here for weeks, you'll be forced to kick your habit. Rafferty won't want to know you. You're an embarrassment to him. You've been collared by the Garda, the Provos will blow you away if you go near the flats. In short, you're not worth a tiddly shit to anyone. What you badly need is a friend.'

Jockey murmured something inaudible.

'By the way,' Carney continued, 'I had a report last night that a girl was looking for you. The nurse on duty said she was very pretty. A girlfriend of yours?'

A cold sweat broke out on Jockey's brow. 'I don't know any girl.'

Carney fumbled in his pocket. 'I nearly forgot. I brought you some cigarettes.'

'You'll have to do better than that.'

'I run a better welfare fund than the Raffertys.'

Jockey winced as he pulled the sheet higher up the bed.

'Just one word. That's all it takes. One piece of information that will put the Raffertys away and you've nothing to worry about.'

'Piss off.'

'You won't get a better offer from anyone else. I could let the word out that you've been indiscreet.'

Jockey threw the clothes back and raised himself on the pillow. 'You wouldn't do that.'

'It's an awful risk to take.'

Maire Brady adjusted her skirt, tightening the belt to allow for the inch she had lost in the last few weeks. The face staring back at her in the mirror was pale, the nose pinched and pointed, the neck shrinking into the shoulders as though some unseen weight was pressing down on it.

Beneath her thin blouse, her emaciated body clearly showed her rib cage. The hands that moved at her waist trembled with a will of their own and she had difficulty keeping her balance on the high-heeled shoes. As she tidied her hair, she wondered how long it would be before the Garda traced her through Jockey.

Callaghan saw her come in and recognised her from the previous night. He took her order for a drink as she sat at the bar. He knew immediately that she was a user. Her face was drawn and her hands would not keep still.

'Meeting your friend again?'

Maire started at the sound of his voice. 'What friend?'

'I saw you last night. You and he had a lot to drink. I thought you might be celebrating something. Is he your boyfriend?'

'No . . . well . . .'

'Crowd's not so big tonight. Tends to be like this when supplies are difficult to get.'

Maire jumped, spilling some of her drink on the counter. Callaghan reached for a cloth, wiping the sticky mixture.

'I think I can help you out.'
'How?'
'You know how.'

Maire surveyed the kitchen behind the bar. A small sink stood in the corner, a bar of soap and a dishcloth lying on the stainless steel draining board. Printed towels hung on pegs, the faint smell of beer rising from them as they dried. Maire picked up a handbag off the single wooden chair and placed it on the table. Music shook the floorboards as she sat down. The flashing lights were further fragmented by the half-open door, reminding her of a scene from a film where Michael Caine was being brainwashed.

She could sense and sometimes see Callaghan moving about the bar. Her anxiety had eased since he made her the offer and she only hoped she would not have to wait until the disco closed before he kept his promise.

As the minutes slipped by, she felt the first pangs of physical discomfort. Pacing the room she tried to stall the onset of cramps. Callaghan was at the tables, talking to a group of men. When the first real pains hit her, she made a decision. Crouching down to the level of the counter, she crept to the till and opened it, her hands trembling as she lifted the spring-loaded catch in the drawer. The deafening blare from the loudspeakers blotted out the sound of the register as she removed a fistful of notes.

Callaghan was still engrossed with his customers as she ducked under the hatch. With her heart thumping, she skipped down the stairs and headed for the station.

'That's blackmail,' Jockey said.

'Look on it as a piece of encouragement. You can hobble about on crutches for the rest of your life or you can be sensible.'

Jockey turned his face to the wall. The Raffertys would have no use for him now. There would be no anonymity on the streets with a damaged leg. He would spend the rest of his life as a misfit and there were those who would take revenge on him.

Jockey turned to face the Inspector, leaning forward to whisper in his ear. 'It would be a one-off deal. I want a ticket to a country of my choice, enough money to set me up for life and a concrete identity.'

Carney opened his eyes wide in amazement.

'I have information that would put Brendan Rafferty and his brother away for life. You could have them on a murder charge.'

'Murder?'

'Slaughterhouse 9.'

Carney's heart skipped a beat.

'You think about it for a while,' said Jockey. 'I can wait.'

Carney stood up slowly. Out in the corridor he paused by the duty officer's chair. 'I don't want anyone going into that room unless they've been cleared personally by me. Is that understood?'

'Yes, sir. No visitors.'

Hurrying to his car, Carney picked up the radio and called the office. 'Fitzgerald? I want Daly to meet me at the Prosecutor's office in half an hour.'

Not waiting for a reply, he replaced the radio on the hook and swung the car in a wide arc, causing oncoming traffic to screech to a halt.

CHAPTER FIFTEEN

Dublin, Wednesday June 6th

The Director of Prosecutions and McQuillan sat opposite Carney and Daly, a thin cloud of tobacco smoke spiralling above their heads.

'Did this Jockey character play a part in the murder?' asked McQuillan.

'He must have something more than hearsay knowledge,' said Carney. 'I know he's close to the family. He's one of their top pushers. He might even organise some of their safe houses.'

'But the carving?' asked the Director. 'Is he likely to have played a part in the carving?'

'I don't think so. My guess is that he was on the lookout for rival pushers and put the finger on the dead man for the Raffertys.'

'No,' said the Director, slowly shaking his head. 'Thinking so and guessing won't be enough. Sure, we can make some sort of deal with him if he gives us evidence that helps put away the Raffertys, but certainly not anything like the deal he's looking for. *And* before there's any talk of deals you'll have to know the degree of his involvement. *And* his uncorroborated evidence won't get us a conviction. He'll need to lead us to some back-up evidence, forensic evidence, something that will stand up in court. Has Byrne made any progress in that area yet?'

'The Murder Squad has been all over the house,' said Carney, 'and they've talked to the Raffertys. So far, nothing. The house was clean, and both Raffertys had alibis.'

Mike McQuillan started to doodle on his pad, then abruptly he closed it. The effects of the two pints of Guinness at lunchtime had given him a headache, and the ploughman's lunch was sitting uneasily in his stomach. 'We do want to get the Raffertys off the streets,' he said to the Director.

The Director narrowed his eyes. 'We also have to consider public reaction if we let this man go free. This was one of the most horrific murders I can remember. I don't think we can let one of the perpetrators float off with an airline ticket and a vast sum of taxpayers' money as a reward for his part in it.'

'What if he didn't take part in it?' asked Carney. 'What if he had no direct connection? Thought the Raffertys just wanted a talk?'

'With the background of the Toman murder, no one is going to believe that.'

A silence descended on the meeting as the Director pushed his chair away from the desk and fiddled with his pipe. Finally he said, 'Can't you just string him along, tell him we're considering it, and try at the same time to get some concrete lead out of him, something we could use in court?'

McQuillan glanced hopefully at Carney, but the Inspector was shaking his head. 'You could give it a try,' said McQuillan.

'I can try it, yes, but I don't see it working.'

'Then all we can do for you,' said the Director, 'is let you offer a deal that falls far short of what he's demanding. If he was, as you suggest, just the man who fingered the victim, and if he's prepared to lead us to evidence that will tie the Raffertys to the murder, then you can offer him an early release deal. I think the Minister for Justice would be prepared to go along with that. If he doesn't fall for you stringing him along, try that deal. You never know, Inspector, he might go for it. Especially if he thinks you're building up a case against him anyway and he's got nothing to lose.'

'Except his life,' said Carney, 'when the Raffertys learn he's turned against them.'

The Director stood up. The meeting was over. 'I'm sorry, Inspector. I know you wanted more than that, but it's the best offer we can make.'

The Grocklesnapper, *Thursday June 7th*

The yacht pitched in the heavy seas, sending a plume of fine white spray leaping over the bow. The wind drove it along the boat, lashing the polished decks. The safety line was out and Taggart hung on tightly, the water splattering off his waterproof cape.

The horizon constantly shifted. The Dutch captain was at the wheel, one arm locked through the spokes, his feet planted well apart. Two of the crew were busy securing the hatches, their faces glistening with salt spray. The coastline of England had disappeared, leaving them surrounded by white-capped waves. Down in the hold, six wooden crates held the consignment of weapons – Kalashnikov rifles with telescopic sights. One of the crates held ammunition. The manifest described them as sporting goods.

Taggart staggered to the rail, hurling his British passport as far as he could. 'How long will it last?' he bellowed.

The captain half turned. 'Once we're round the head it will be better. Maybe another hour.'

The propeller raced as it lifted out of the water. Waves swept under the boat making the timbers groan. The faint outline of another ship appeared to leeward, its course parallel to their own.

'Trawler,' the captain shouted. 'Heading for the Irish coast.'

Taggart fought his way to the cabin, allowing the pitch of the boat to throw him inside.

It was some time after the wind abated that Taggart felt comfortable again. His inner ear still pitched and rolled despite the calmer seas.

The captain fiddled with the tuner of the short-band radio, the static crackling in the confined space.

'Is it calm enough to make the transfer?' Taggart asked.

'Ja. We can make the transfer.'

Taggart looked at his watch. In three hours time it would be seven o'clock in the evening and they would be seventy miles off the Irish coast. Allowing two hours for the reloading, they should make land by two in the morning. By daybreak, the guns should be well on their way to the border.

They sighted the boat on the horizon. The anchor was tossed over the side, the barnacle-encrusted chains grating as they fell into the sea.

'Definitely a fishing vessel,' the captain announced, handing the binoculars to Taggart.

'How soon before she's alongside?'

'Thirty minutes. No more. We'll bring her round to the port side and let her load directly from the hatches. Are you coming back with us?'

Taggart thought for a moment. 'No. I'll leave you.'

The trawler came on station, rubber tyres scraping the side of the yacht. Ropes were thrown and the vessels secured. Taggart watched from the deck as the lifting gear swung into place. The captain kept one eye on the radar for other ships in the area, leaving the crew to get on with their work.

Blue smoke drifted up from the coughing motor as the crates were raised over the rail. Taggart wiped salt water from his face, rubbing his eyes with his knuckles to ease the stinging sensation. At 8.20 the last of the crates disappeared into the hold of the trawler and men with shovels bent their backs, covering the load with fish. The smell turned Taggart's stomach. He paid the captain and walked to the stern. Two men, their thick woollen sweaters smeared with oil and grease, waved to him, signalling him over the side. He stepped on the rail, allowing them to grab him by the arms, and he was hauled onto the trawler.

As night closed in, the two vessels disengaged, the fishing boat moving westwards to the steady thump of its powerful diesel engines. Taggart watched until the yacht was a dot on the horizon.

They ploughed through the waves in a slow, rhythmic motion. The running lights were off and the cloud cover provided a protective shroud. He tried unsuccessfully to sleep, joining the rest of the crew on deck as midnight approached.

In the early hours, the captain called from the cabin, his arm pointing to the shore where two lights winked on and off. The captain replied, swinging a storm lantern in a steady arc.

On the beach, the lorry's engine was started and it reversed along the metal slats to the water's edge. The driver joined his colleagues on the sand, helping to place the roller bars into position.

Behan gazed in amazement at the man who was first to clamber ashore, the man who called himself Taggart. 'Good God,' he whispered to himself, 'it's Crowe.' Then he raced forward, hand outstretched. 'We didn't expect you on the boat. Welcome home, Michael.'

Dublin, Thursday June 7th

Sean Rafferty was in the bathroom when he heard his brother call. It came over more as a shout for help than a simple request for his presence and he fumbled with his trousers, stumbling as he lurched for the door. Rose was on the landing, a worried expression on her face.

'What's it about this time?' he asked. Ignoring him, she entered the bathroom and locked the door behind her. She wanted no part of this latest crisis.

Brendan was pacing the room. 'That miserable little bastard,' he spat as Sean joined him. 'That lousy little creep.'

'The old fella at the flats? The one who set Jockey up? I told you, that'll be taken care of.' He gave Brendan a wide berth, perching himself on the arm of a chair, a hand nervously brushing through his hair.

'No, you bloody idiot!' Brendan shouted. 'Not him! Take care of him, yes. Then take care of Jockey. He's your bloody man and you can deal with him.'

Sean looked up in surprise. 'What about Jockey? He's in hospital.'

'I know he's in fucking hospital. What you have to do is make sure he never gets out.'

CHAPTER SIXTEEN

Dublin, Friday June 8th

Mad Johnny studied the form from the papers on the wall of the Sean Graham betting office, scratching his head from time to time as the small print blurred. The results service and commentary were testing in the background, causing a further distraction. Counting the money in his pocket, he calculated that he could afford no more than two pounds on the whole of the day's racing, which meant his winnings would hardly change his lifestyle. One day he knew he would hit it big. Until that day came he was determined never to miss a chance of supplementing his income. It never occurred to him that he could do that by simply giving up the horses altogether. Scribbling down the names of three runners at the Epsom meeting, he wrote out his modest bet, already looking forward to watching the races on television.

After making his usual grumble at the 20 per cent betting tax, he buttoned his jacket and took a wary glance at the sky. At his age he had to watch his health. It had been a trip to the betting shop during a rainstorm that had nearly cost him his life, going down with a chest virus two days after the soaking and needing hospital treatment in an oxygen tent. He was more careful now.

The four-hundred-yard walk across the derelict ground and the side streets brought him to the rear entrance to the flats in six minutes, allowing for a stop to look in the window of a bicycle shop.

He had been toying with the idea of saving for a bike for the best part of a year. In his younger days he had been a fine cyclist, touring the country lanes and hills around his uncle's farm in Wicklow. Now his enthusiasm was tempered by a fear of the traffic which roared past the entrance to the flats and a sneaking suspicion that, as most of his journeys on it would be to the pub, the chances of surviving the return trip were stacked against him. Nevertheless, he loved the shop with its display of shiny frames and polished wheels. The designs had changed a lot since his youth, the handlebars at seemingly impossible angles, and the gears a mass of complicated technology. The advertising posters showed boys of ten or eleven doing wheelies, bikes off the ground, heads covered with gaily coloured crash helmets. Mad Johnny doubted the sanity of today's generation.

At the rear of the flats he paused to catch his breath. Every time he made the trip, the place where he had to stop for a breather seemed a shorter and shorter distance from his starting point. Last week he could distinctly remember reaching the courtyard.

A large man was leaning against the wall reading a paper, a cigarette dangling from the corner of his mouth. He looked up as Mad Johnny approached and Mad Johnny nodded absently.

The entrance to the ground-floor flat was shaded, making it difficult for him to see as he fumbled in his pocket for the key. The key was attached to a gold chain, the watch that went with it long since pawned to pay for his drinking. He scraped the metal surround several times before the key slipped into the lock. As he turned it, the shadows deepened and he sensed a presence behind him.

At first he thought the man must be lost. The figure towering above him was a stranger, at least six foot, with a scar running from the bridge of his nose to the corner of his mouth.

An arm snaked out and grabbed Mad Johnny by the neck, the pressure from the hand increasing as Mad Johnny began to struggle. Gurgling noises came from his throat as he twisted to escape the crushing grip. His only thought was that the stranger had made a mistake. Any minute he expected to be released and told the nature of the joke. When the man started to punch him in the stomach with his free hand, driving the last drops of breath from his body, Mad Johnny realised that this was it. His eyes pleaded with the man for an explanation, some reason that would justify his premature end.

The man recognised the look on his victim's face, nodding slowly in understanding. 'Hello,' he said, by way of explanation. 'My name's Charlie.'

Dublin, Friday June 8th

'Nothing on the lists,' Carney said, tossing the papers to Daly. 'No stolen passports to match with the names. Sweet F.A. from the immigration people. It's beginning to look as if our friend decided not to come or else came in via the North.'

'Why not let it go?' Daly suggested. 'The drug business is only a temporary thing.'

Carney made an impatient gesture with his hand. 'Don't you realise that this could be the key to everything else. If we can trace the drugs and their pushers we can trace Crowe, and if we can get to him it just might stop a new terrorist organisation in its tracks.'

Daly seemed unconvinced but Carney pushed on. 'You're as bad as Devlin. He thinks this will all blow over. If a significant amount of drugs enters the market they have to expand the users. What happens when they pull out? Heroin isn't a take-it-or-leave-it proposition. Those users will have to demand supplies from elsewhere and Rafferty will step in.'

'Get rid of Rafferty,' Daly suggested. 'Let Crowe go and fight his war in the North.'

'If I thought you were serious I'd boot you out now,' Carney said, unable to hide his impatience.

The telephone rang and Carney answered. He nodded as he took the message, swivelling the pad round so that Daly could share the news. 'How long ago was this?'

'Let's go,' he said to Daly.

Daly drove, picking his way through the traffic, heading towards the Green and Grafton Street beyond. 'Nice of Byrne to tell us,' Daly commented, jamming on the brakes to avoid a car in front that dived into one of the parking spaces.

'Might be wrong,' Carney said thoughtfully, 'but I wouldn't mind betting that the victim is the one who put the word out on Jockey.'

'Then we're talking about Rafferty again,' said Daly. 'Maybe it'll be a break for us. If Rafferty keeps dumping bodies on the Commissioner's doorstep the Director of Prosecutions may be forced to give way on a deal with Jockey.'

'Don't bet your pension on it,' said Carney. 'We've had the Director's final offer. If we're to get the Raffertys it's going to have to be through sheer bloody effort on our part. I don't think we can rely on help from anybody else.'

Aughrim, Friday June 8th

The sound of an engine starting woke Crowe from a deep sleep. He had to strain to raise his eyelids, his limbs stiff and leaden as he tried to stir himself from the makeshift bed of mattress and sheets. The sound of men talking drifted in from the area to the back of the old farm and it slowly came to him where he was and what was going on. Raising himself on one elbow he glanced at his wristwatch, glad to see that he had managed five hours sleep. A twittering erupted on the roof and he heard the scratching of birds in the rotting eaves.

As the lorry changed gear, rumbling its way to the road, he swung his legs off the bed, pausing to rub the wound which ran several inches down his calf.

The water in the tap was brackish, running in a muddy brown stream into the stained basin of the sink. He braved the shivering fit that swept over him as he splashed water on his face and neck. The pot on the stove was lukewarm and the coffee had a stale, musty smell. Ignoring it he took a salt biscuit from a packet on the window ledge and slowly chewed it, watching the men coming in from the field.

Behan led them, a thick pullover with a high neck shielding him from the worst of the wind. The other men trailed a little way behind, stopping every now and then to look down the road at the departing vehicle.

Three of them sat round the table. Behan picked at the loose skin on his hand caused by the rough edges of the crates.

'Should be there in three hours,' he said to break the silence.

Crowe tapped his fingers on the wooden surface, his tongue working at the roof of his mouth to dislodge the remains of his breakfast.

'Any problems?' he asked when the other man had left.

'No. I heard that Liam was in trouble last night. He went back to Dundalk and had some problems in a bar.'

Crowe bit his lip hard. 'Where is he now?'

'The Garda booked him and let him go.'

'Did he give them an address?'

'I don't know.' Behan was sorry he had mentioned the incident. 'Some of the lads were talking about it this morning. I think Davy was with him last night for part of the time.'

'I told them all to lay low,' said Crowe.

Behan just shrugged, rising from his chair, eager to be out in the fresh air again.

'If you see him before I do,' Crowe called as Behan opened the door, 'tell him I was asking for him.'

CHAPTER SEVENTEEN

Dublin, Friday June 8th

The hospital laundry was on the second floor at the back of the building away from the wards. Large skips on rubber wheels were parked at strategic points along the corridors and chutes ran down from the upper floors to the laundry itself. Most of the items consigned to the official receptacles were linen for the beds but there were several doctors on the staff who had an arrangement with the supervisor, and they dropped their coats in to be cleaned.

At this time of night the laundry was closed, a lone attendant watching over the gleaming vats and the simmering boilers that fretted on standby, waiting for the morning shift to revive them. Most of the skips were empty but Boyle persevered, padding quietly along the highly polished tiles, searching in every basket. He found a coat, but the jacket was creased and seemed to be at least one size too small. He held on to it nevertheless, continuing his foraging in the hope that something more suitable would turn up.

On the floor above, Garda Smyth tried to stop himself from yawning, placing the back of his hand over his mouth. He had read the paperback twice already and was thoroughly bored. To relieve the monotony he walked over to the private ward and peered in. The patient was lying on his side and appeared to be asleep. Smyth stretched, scratching his ample stomach and wishing it were midnight so he could go home to his supper of meatloaf.

Boyle slipped into the toilets and chose a cubicle at the far end. He had a choice of two coats, both of which were small. He selected the least rumpled of the two, leaving the jacket open. Making sure the toilet was empty, he emerged from the stall and viewed himself in the long mirror, straightening his tie and half turning to see the length of the jacket at the back. Folding the discarded coat neatly, he returned to the corridor, dropping it in the first skip he saw.

The majority of the visitors for the evening session had left, but a few lingered, the nurses tolerantly leaving them for as long as they wanted. A ginger-haired staff nurse was in the dispensary with a junior, checking the little plastic cups on a trolley and matching them with the doctor's prescriptions.

Boyle passed the main surgical ward and turned right at the bottom of the corridor to where three private rooms were closed off to the general view. The Garda was just taking his seat again, a weary expression on his face. He revived a little when the man with the doctor's coat approached, and sat upright in the chair, his manner suddenly businesslike.

'Good evening officer,' Boyle said, stopping outside the door. 'Everything okay?'

'All quiet,' the Garda said, trying to remember if he had seen the ginger-haired, freckled doctor before.

'Just want to check his leg,' Boyle said, walking into the room.

The Garda racked his brain, but the man did not come to mind. They changed the staff so much, he supposed it was hardly surprising that a new face should appear from time to time. Still, there was something that bothered him, something that he could not quite put his finger on.

Boyle walked over to the bed, thankful that his victim was asleep. They had never met before but it saved all the playacting. Taking a quick glance over his shoulder he picked up the spare pillow from the bedside locker, gripping the edges firmly. He reckoned twenty seconds would be enough to choke the life out of a drowsy man. The biggest problem was to keep him quiet.

Garda Smyth still had a vague feeling that something was not quite right. He prided himself on being observant. To keep his memory sharp he constantly practised the art, noting the clothes, the colour of hair, the approximate height, and the general bearing of everyone he met. It made up for his lack of fleet-footedness and his tendency to overweight.

Stethoscope, he thought suddenly. The doctor did not have a

stethoscope protruding from his jacket . . . or a name tag. Concerned, he rose from his chair, then hesitated. Stethoscopes weren't welded onto doctors. Why shouldn't a doctor appear without one?

Boyle made his way steadily round the foot of the bed, anxious not to have to stretch when he made his move. It was essential that his movements were smooth and precise. If he timed it right, the victim would be half dead before he awoke. He judged the distance carefully, holding the pillow in place. With his hand in a position on the pillow that would allow him to exert maximum pressure on the nose and mouth, he leaned forward. For a split second nothing happened. Then he felt the first stirrings beneath his hand. Putting the full force of his body behind his arm, he pressed with all his strength. The muffled noises from beneath the pillow were almost inaudible in the room, only the convulsive jerking of the legs causing Boyle concern. Sliding sideways he fell on the damaged leg.

'What the hell's going on?' Smyth shouted from the door.

Boyle sprang back in surprise, then hurled the pillow at the officer. Smyth flung out an arm. As he did so he felt a sharp pain in the groin, then a dull blow to his neck. Throwing aside the pillow, he was in time to see the man racing from the room, his open jacket flapping as he ran.

On the bed, Jockey was writhing in agony, clutching his shattered leg, his screams bringing the hospital to life, nurses running towards the sound. Smyth rushed to the door but the attacker was gone. A nurse brushed past him into the room. She made straight for the figure in the bed.

'What have you done to him?' she asked angrily as Smyth staggered in to help.

Carney flexed his muscles and admired the result in the bathroom mirror. Despite his lack of regular exercise he had held his shape well and was thankful for the legacy of his younger days when he had been sports mad. All he managed now was the occasional round of golf with his nextdoor neighbour or an infrequent trip to the lake for a spot of fishing. There were so many other things he would like to do, but he ruefully dismissed them from his mind.

Mary was propped up on the pillow, the phrase book held out to the bedside light.

'*¿Adonde es el cuarto de baño? Me llamo Maria.*'

'Very good,' Carney said, climbing into bed. 'What does it mean?'

'My name is Mary. Where is the bathroom?'

'Why do you have to tell them your name to use the bathroom?'

She hit him on the head with the book. 'It's always useful to know a few phrases.'

'I found in France that if they thought you could speak the lingo, they just rabbited on and made no attempt at English.'

'You really are a cynic,' she told him. '*¿Adonde es el café?*'

'Half the people who run establishments in Spain are English.'

'This is for the other half,' she retorted, determined not to be put off. Half the enjoyment of a holiday was the anticipation and preparation. 'How long does it take to fly to Spain?'

'About two, two and a half hours I should imagine. Why?'

'Aren't you looking forward to it?'

'I haven't had time to think about it. There's a lot going on.'

'I have a lot going on and I can't think of anything else,' she said, dreamily.

'Put the light out.'

'You really are growing up to be an old grouch,' she said, tugging at the cord.

Downstairs the telephone rang again.

'Sod that bloody phone,' Mary said, covering her ears with the pillow. 'Tell them you're out.'

Carney padded softly down to the hall and picked up the receiver in his right hand, jamming it between his shoulder and chin.

'We have a problem,' Walsh said at the other end. 'Someone tried to put our witness to sleep.'

Carney parked outside the front entrance to the hospital. As he crossed the road he buttoned his coat, in an attempt to hide his hastily-thrown-on clothes. The night was cold and a chill wind hurried him up the hospital steps to the warmth of the reception area.

Walsh met him in the passage leading to the lifts. 'Just arrived?'

Carney nodded, pushing the call button. 'What exactly happened?'

'I only know what I told you on the phone.'

They made their way to the third floor where a sister checked their identities. The door to Jockey's room was closed. Garda Smyth stood outside with his replacement and two detectives from the Murder Squad. Walsh approached the four men. 'Have any of you talked to him yet?'

'Just briefly,' a detective replied. 'The doctor is in with him now. He's in a lot of pain.'

'You were on duty, Smyth?'

'Yes, sir.'

After Smyth had finished his account of what happened, Carney took Walsh by the arm, leading him to a row of chairs outside the matron's office. 'This is a real bloody mess,' he said.

'We'll have him moved and put an extra man on guard.'

'I don't think you understand. Someone tipped off Rafferty.'

Walsh was startled. 'Why would . . .'

'Because someone told him that Jockey had offered to talk.'

'That's not possible. The only people who knew about it were you, me, Daly, the Prosecutor's office and the Commissioner.'

'Yes. Gives you the shivers, doesn't it?'

CHAPTER EIGHTEEN

Dublin, Saturday June 9th

An orderly wheeled Jockey into the lift, a nurse standing by holding the drip clear of the trolley. Carney followed them in with Garda Smyth and pushed the 'door close' button with his thumb.

On the top floor all the corridors were empty, the staff working behind hermetically sealed partitions in the laboratories that served the hospital complex. At the far end the orderly stopped and waited until the nurse pushed open a door. The room was small, with one little window high up near the ceiling. The walls were covered with electrical sockets and Carney guessed that it had once served for research of some kind.

Instead of laboratory equipment, a bed had been placed against the wall beneath the window, in full sight of the corridor outside, and a bell-push had been rigged, linking the room directly to the sister's office two floors below.

While they were transferring Jockey to the bed, Carney went out to check the placement of the chairs that would accommodate the two guards Walsh had authorised. One sat directly opposite the room, the other to the left of the lift covering the stairs.

'You check everyone,' Carney said to Smyth as the nurse and orderly left.

Smyth nodded solemnly. 'You did a good job last night,' said Carney.

Walsh was in the sister's office when Carney arrived and he gave Carney a warning nod.

'Sorry about this,' Carney said immediately, taking his cue. 'I think Superintendent Walsh has explained the gravity of the situation and until the doctor says he can be moved I'm afraid we'll have to settle where we are. The two officers will keep out of the way, but I must stress that the staff in attendance will have to be identified. If anyone tries to enter and has not been cleared with them they will be refused permission.'

The sister nodded. 'We'll have to make the best of it,' she answered with a smile. 'I've briefed certain of the staff on the situation. Hopefully it won't last too long.'

'Have you any idea how long?' Walsh asked.

'You know he has a drug addiction on top of his gunshot wounds?' the sister said. Carney and Walsh nodded. 'If everything goes well and the leg heals, I would guess three to four weeks.'

'Before you'll let us move him?' asked Walsh.

'Oh, yes,' the sister said. 'He's a very sick young man.'

The two men stayed in the reception area until the second Garda arrived.

'Gives us time to work out a deal,' Carney said, trying to offer some consolation.

Walsh chewed his bottom lip nervously. 'Gives Rafferty time to make another move as well.'

'Can't we hold them on anything?'

Walsh lit a cigarette, then remembered where he was. Taking Carney by the arm, he ushered him out onto the steps. 'We're checking now to see if there's anything outstanding. Fines, parking tickets, but it's a hopeless chance.'

They walked in silence to the car, Carney slightly ahead, his hands buried deep in the pockets of his raincoat. 'About the other problem . . .'

Walsh slid into the car on the driver's side and reached over to unlock the passenger door. When Carney was settled next to him he considered the matter. 'Who knew about it in your department besides yourself and Daly?'

'No one else.'

'What about hospital staff? Were any of them in the room when you were talking to Jockey, a nurse perhaps . . .?'

Carney shook his head. 'The only people outside the force who knew were those at the meeting, McQuillan and the Director.'

'You trust Daly?'

Carney looked at Walsh. 'Yes.'

'What a mess,' Walsh said, unable to accept the alternative. 'Is there anything we can use as a cross-check?'

'I'll certainly check for anything suspicious but it might be better if we set something up.'

'Like what?'

'Like we'll feed the same people some erroneous details about our future plans for Jockey and see if it gets back to Rafferty.'

'You think you can handle it?'

Carney nodded. 'I think something can be arranged.'

'Where should I drop you?' Walsh asked, starting the engine.

'Drop me at Trinity. I have some shopping to do. I'll walk from there.'

'Buying yourself a new raincoat at last?' Walsh asked with a chuckle.

'A pair of swimming trunks,' Carney replied, without further explanation.

Aughrim, Saturday June 9th

Crowe raised the rifle to his shoulder and closed one eye as he squinted down the sight. The cross-hairs bisected the tin can and Crowe squeezed gently on the trigger. The recoil was minimal. The shot echoed off the surrounding hills, sending sheep scattering. The sheep followed a leader to the lower ground, congregating in a group by the stone wall. As the sound died away, an uneasy peace returned and they started to graze again.

The hole in the can was slightly left of centre, the entry point small compared to the torn and twisted metal where the bullet had exited. Using a fine-bladed penknife, Crowe adjusted the small screw at the base of the sights and then retraced his footsteps, returning to the same spot, where he took aim and fired again. This time the sheep panicked, splitting into several groups, charging in all directions and not stopping until they were at the far ends of the field.

Crowe nodded in satisfaction. The can was neatly pierced through the centre.

Behan stood at the door of the farmhouse, leaning heavily on the cold outer wall. Crowe had been practising for nearly an hour and it was beginning to show in the surrounding countryside. The birds could not settle on their nests in the copse and they wheeled overhead in twittering flocks, the sheep had scattered and the cattle in the field at the back were lowing loudly, their hooves pawing the wet grass. To the east, the cars on the road now seemed closer than ever and Behan was sure that the drivers could hear the gunfire.

It was only when Crowe shouldered the rifle and tossed the tin can into the ditch that Behan relaxed, but he was still fearful of the mood that would greet him when Crowe returned.

'A fine weapon,' Crowe shouted as he jumped the ditch.

Behan smiled. 'I was worried,' he admitted. 'The animals were getting jumpy.'

Crowe cocked his head to one side. 'Worried? No need for that. No one will disturb us up here.'

To prove his point, he took aim and fired. Behan saw the sheep turn frantically, their distress obvious. As they rushed up the field, Behan noticed one of them lying motionless.

'Mutton for supper,' Crowe said, a huge grin on his face.

The lorry slowed down to let the car behind pass, the driver lowering the window to signal that the road was clear. Waiting until the car had disappeared, the lorry turned right into the concealed entrance, bumping its way over the hardening ruts to the farmhouse behind the trees.

Two hundred yards from the house, the driver sounded the horn and flashed his headlights. Crowe peeped through the curtains.

'He's back,' he announced to Behan, who was pouring himself his third drink of the evening.

The kitchen sink was smeared with blood, the stripped carcass of the sheep lying along the draining board, its head severed.

The driver parked the lorry at the back of the house, locked the cab and walked round the front to where Crowe waited for him at the door.

'All delivered?'

The driver handed the keys to Crowe. 'Went without a hitch,' he said, wrinkling his nose as he entered the house. 'God, what's that smell?'

'Dennis has been preparing a meal,' said Crowe. Behan raised his eyes heavenwards as he caught the driver's glance, but said nothing.

'Did you deliver everything?' Crowe asked.

'I told you,' the driver replied, taking a seat away from the kitchen, 'it all went as planned.'

Crowe stood with his back to the table, staring at the driver. 'I heard you've been a naughty boy,' he said, picking up the rifle. The driver looked puzzled. He shrugged. 'You had a run in with the Garda.'

The driver rubbed the palm of his hand down his leather jacket, scratching it against the zip. 'It was nothing,' he said.

Crowe snapped the breach open, letting it go with a sudden click. The driver pretended to ignore the movement. 'What's been happening here?' he asked Behan.

Behan was watching Crowe, unable to make up his mind what was going on. 'Nothing much,' he answered carefully, his eyes on the gun. 'We had some shooting practice.'

'I also heard,' Crowe continued, 'that it's not the first time.'

The driver looked closely at Behan for some indication of the situation but Behan averted his gaze, suddenly finding the empty grate of interest.

'There was no harm done. Just an argument,' the driver said.

'Can't afford any weak links,' Crowe said casually.

'For Christ's sake, I had an argument in a pub, that's all.'

'Some argument.' Crowe squeezed the trigger. 'When you're feeling up to it,' he said to the trembling Behan, 'bury him somewhere out of sight.'

He walked to the door, lifting the catch with the barrel of the gun. He paused on the step as the cold wind enveloped him. 'I never liked Liam,' he said, before vanishing into the night.

Dublin, Saturday June 9th

Maire was in agony. The cramps in her stomach doubled her up and she was beginning to draw suspicious glances from the passengers as they made their way to the trains. Boyle watched from the shadow of the toilets, smiling every now and then at the girl's discomfort. He waited another five minutes before stepping out into the stream of commuters.

Maire clutched her sides and bit her lip in an attempt to stem the nausea. Her vision was beginning to blur and she knew she would collapse if help did not arrive quickly.

'You look ill,' the voice at her side said.

Maire instinctively tried to turn away.

'It's okay. I can help you.'

Maire felt a hand on her arm, pushing her gently towards the street.

'Do you live far away?'

She shook her head. 'About ten minutes.'

Boyle followed a few yards behind as the girl half walked, half stumbled through the maze of poorly lit side streets. He took the key from her hand and opened the door wide. He glanced in both directions before following her to the basement flat. The musty smell stung his nostrils as he entered the bedroom. A stained mattress lay in one corner and unwashed dishes littered the floor.

Taking off his coat, he flung it to one side. Maire snatched the packet from his hand and carried it to the table where she prepared the syringe. He turned away as she injected the drug into her thigh. When he turned to face her again, she was lying naked on the mattress, her eyes closed, one arm across her stomach, the other bent at right angles above her head.

Maire moaned as the knee was pressed into her stomach. A hand gripped her shoulders and pushed down as she tried to scramble away.

She tried to calm him with soothing words, rubbing her hand along the side of his face. He slapped it away, straddling her, his fist smashing into her nose. Blood spurted over the floor and she began to choke. When she finally blacked out, Boyle relaxed, sweat dripping from his forehead.

He wiped blood from the back of his hand with a handkerchief, stuffing the soiled piece of cotton into the girl's mouth. Taking a deep breath, he removed the knife from his back pocket and opened the blade.

The girl came to life, struggling and thrashing as he started to cut away her bottom lip.

CHAPTER NINETEEN

Dublin, Sunday June 10th

The telephone rang shrilly in the hall.

'Tell them he's not in,' Mary called as Sinead answered it. Carney took the phone from his daughter.

'Something of interest,' Walsh told him. 'A girl by the name of Maire Brady has just been admitted to the General. Badly mutilated about the face. Apparently she was only conscious for a few minutes and they're operating now. All she could say was Jockey's name.'

'Okay. I'm on my way.'

'Can't you ever say *no*?' Mary asked, handing him his coat. 'It's Sunday.'

'I have to go to the hospital.'

Mary kissed him on the cheek. 'Try not to be too long.'

It was warm in the car and Carney opened the window. He tried to fit the latest news into place as he drove through the traffic. It was possible that the girl was the same one who had tried to visit Jockey earlier. Probably one of his users. Maybe even his girlfriend. Someone may have had a go at her to warn Jockey. By the time he reached the hospital, his head was full of half-completed theories. Two Garda officers met him in reception and gave him brief details of the case.

'Do we know if she has any family in Dublin?' Carney asked.

'Not yet. We found a few papers on her. She has a student card. The station is trying to get in touch with the university.'

'You might as well carry on.'

'Will the Drug Squad be handling the case?'

'Most likely. If there's any change, I'll get in touch.'

It was two hours before Maire was wheeled out of the theatre, a doctor and two nurses in attendance. Carney showed his card and was led to an empty office.

'Can you tell me what happened?' he said.

The doctor scratched his chin. 'From the wounds I would say she was attacked by a straight razor or an extremely sharp knife. The cuts appear to be deliberate. One ear has been partially severed and her bottom lip was cut away. All the damage is confined to her face.'

'Will she survive?'

'From the initial examination it appears she is a drug user. Probably heroin. Her arms and thighs are covered with needle tracks. I really can't say at this stage what the prognosis will be.'

'When can I talk to her?'

'She'll be out for at least eight hours. You might get something out of her then, but you can only have a few minutes.'

'Can't you do anything right?' Brendan Rafferty shouted. 'Can't any of you do anything right?'

Tony Boyle stood before him, saying nothing. He had already had his say, how it hadn't been his fault that the Garda had burst into the room, how at least he had escaped without being identified.

Sean Rafferty sat at the far side of the room, close to his wife. He looked as if he hoped that distance would keep him out of range of his brother's temper.

'And this freelance job you did for Callaghan,' roared Brendan. 'What sort of crazy bloody cock-up was that? Carving up a user, putting her in hospital where Carney can have a chat with her any time he bloody pleases? As if Carney wasn't giving us enough trouble without this fucking madness to add to it.' He stepped closer to Boyle and jabbed a forefinger at the man's chest. 'You're finished. You hear me? Finished! Why I ever bothered to take on a witless moron like you in the first place, I'll never know.'

When Boyle had gone he rounded on his brother. 'Leave things to you, eh? And you decide to use Boyle. And it was your job to look after the pushers. And what happens? You trust Jockey with the locations of all the safe houses. That bastard Jockey was your man. Christ, if we ever get through this mess we're in I'm going to pack you off somewhere where you can't do me any more damage, you and that stupid wife of yours.'

'Now, wait just a minute.' Rose started forward angrily. 'Sean, are you going to let him talk to you like that?'

'I'll talk to both of you whatever way I want.'

'What's so important about this Jockey?' she asked. 'What does he know? Why are you so frightened of him talking?'

'It's not your business.'

'It is my business. I'm family,' she said and, when he started to sneer, she added, 'It's more than just the safe houses, isn't it?'

'I'm going out,' he declared and headed for the door. That's right, Rose thought bitterly, run away, as usual.

'He'll get over it,' said Sean, relaxing now that Brendan was out of the house. 'He always does. He just has these moods.'

'Moods!' snorted Rose. 'Good God, Sean, he's vicious.'

'Yeah, he did go overboard with Boyle, throwing him out like that. We need Boyle if we're to make another shot at Jockey. He's loyal, he knows the scene and he can't wait to get back at Carney. Carney gave him a hard time when he was pushing for Flanagan. When Brendan calms down I'll have a word with him about Tony.'

Rose turned on him angrily. 'Forget all that for now. What do we do about Brendan?'

'I just told you . . .'

'I can't take it any more, the way he bullies us.'

'We've no choice, Rose.'

'Maybe,' she said thoughtfully. 'What does Jockey know that frightens him so much? 'It wouldn't have anything to do with the blood on his shirt?'

The colour drained from Sean's face. 'Whose shirt?'

'Brendan's. He left it in the basket, for washing. Over a week ago. Just two or three bloodstains. Maybe he didn't notice them.'

'For God's sake, Rose! What are we going to do?'

'I don't know,' she said. 'I don't know . . . yet.'

Carney sat on the edge of the bed, trying to visualise what the girl looked like beneath the mass of bandages. He checked his watch, thinking he might leave it until the morning. A nurse came in, carrying a stainless steel tray with a small vial and a hypodermic syringe.

'Is there a doctor on duty?' Carney asked.

'Dr Morris is on call.'

Carney thought better of it. The nurse drew the curtains around the bed and Carney watched her silhouette as she administered the injection. 'That was to keep her under,' the nurse said as she was leaving. 'I don't think you'll be able to talk to her tonight.'

Carney waited ten more minutes. Suddenly feeling tired, he left the hospital, toying with the idea of ringing Walsh and disturbing him for a change.

CHAPTER TWENTY

Dublin, Monday June 11th

When Daly entered the office Carney cupped his hand over the phone. 'It's Byrne,' he explained. 'Listen Kevin, I'm going over to the hospital later this morning to talk to Jockey before we move him. I want to finalise our offer.'

Two Gardai walked past the office sharing a joke and Carney waited until the noise subsided. 'Yes, I've decided to move him to the Beechmount Nursing Home in Portmarnock later this week. The doctors say he should be okay to move by Thursday.'

Carney paused. 'Well, I think it will be easier to guard. It's a two-storey building with about a dozen private beds. We'll transfer him early in the morning. I checked it out over the weekend.'

Carney nodded a few times. 'Okay, let's say in half an hour. I'll call by on the way.'

Daly raised his eyebrows as Carney replaced the phone. 'I didn't know he was fit to be moved.'

'The hospital says he's stabilised. We'll see what tubes he still has in him. Probably ask the hospital to arrange it and give the ambulance an escort.'

'Do you want me to come and see Byrne with you?'

'I don't think so,' Carney said. 'What's that you've got there?'

Daly picked up the sheet of paper from the edge of the desk and passed it to Carney. 'It's a list from Special Branch with the names of Crowe's associates.'

Carney scanned the sheet, his features clouding. 'Is that it? Three names and all in custody.'

''Fraid so,' said Daly. 'Doesn't help very much.'

'Anything from Purnell in Belfast?'

'Not a thing. They have no reports of Belfast being used as a conduit for drugs coming into the South.'

'Great!' exclaimed Carney, pushing the paper back to Daly. 'Just great!'

'Any news of that girl?'

'I'm off to see her now,' Carney said, easing himself out of the chair. 'If Walsh is looking for me tell him I'll be back about eleven and no, I haven't spoken to her yet.'

The hospital was crowded. Orderlies wheeled their charges up and down the corridor leading to the X-ray department, mingling with the out-patients and visitors milling about the reception area. To the left a steady stream of walking wounded made its way to the casualty department. Carney wondered how so many accidents could happen in so short a time. He managed to catch the eye of one of the nurses behind the desk. 'Maire Brady.'

The nurse flicked through the pages of a tattered ledger. 'Second floor now,' she informed him, returning to deal with a small child who was playing with a ball amidst the wheelchairs.

Carney decided that the exercise would do him good. Ignoring the queue at the lift, he skirted the crowds and began to take the steps two at a time. A nurse directed him to the small room at the end of the ward, telling him he could have five minutes. Inside, a bed lay against the far wall, a locker and a table to the left and a chair to the right. Maire was propped upright, her face masked by clean white bandages that covered her from forehead to chin. A slit had been left across her eyes and Carney noticed the eyes move as he entered.

'I'm Inspector Carney,' he said. He sat down and pulled the chair close to the bed. Maire looked away and he thought he saw tears form and trickle beneath the bandages. 'Can you talk?' he asked her gently.

There was no reply, just the faint sound of sobbing and a tremor from the bed as Maire's body began to shake.

'You're in good hands,' he said, patting her arm. 'The doctor says he can patch you up good as new. It's also a chance to kick the habit.'

Maire let her head drift to the pillow, from which she looked at him through the bandages.

'We have a surprise for you,' Carney said. 'Your friend Jockey is in the hospital with you. When you're better we can arrange for you to see him.'

He sensed an effort on the girl's part. She slowly raised herself on her elbow and turned her face towards him.

'I hope he dies,' she whispered harshly, and her head fell back onto the pillow.

Carney closed the door, isolating the room from the bustle of the hospital, and strode purposefully to the foot of the bed, where he towered over Jockey.

'You really are a little weasel, aren't you?' he said, his hands stuffed in his jacket pockets to stop them shaking. 'I think you'd better tell me everything about your activities with the Raffertys before we talk a deal. I'd like to know just how much I'll have to sweep under the carpet when you've gone.'

'What the hell are you talking about?' Jockey asked.

'Maire Brady is in a hospital bed a few floors below you. Does that jog your memory?'

'Look, Carney, she was a user I supplied. That's all.'

'How would you like it if I jumped on your leg?' Carney said, moving to the side of the bed.

Jockey's face contorted in terror, the very thought sending a sickly feeling washing over him. His left arm shot out and he fumbled for the bell-push. Carney caught him by the wrist. 'I want to know the connection,' he said, his face set in a grim stare, the pressure on Jockey's wrist increasing.

'You mad bastard, let go of me!' Jockey cried, attempting to wriggle to the far side of the bed.

Sharp stabbing pains began to shoot from his knee up the inside of his thigh and he stopped struggling, the pain from his leg blocking out the threat from Carney.

Releasing him, Carney took a handkerchief from his back pocket and wiped his brow. 'Now you tell me everything,' he said in a calmer voice, 'or the deal's off.'

Jockey waved a hand in submission, drawing in deep breaths, fighting the pain. Carney sat down, waiting for the crisis to be over, his eyes never leaving Jockey's face.

'She used to put out for me in exchange for the dope,' Jockey began casually, dismissing the fact as of no consequence.

'What do you mean,' Carney asked, 'put out for you? What the hell does that mean?'

Jockey shrugged. 'She used to do it instead of giving me money.'

'And?'

'And that's about it.' Jockey watched Carney carefully for any sudden movement.

'Nice try,' Carney said, patting him on the arm. 'Now try again and this time is the last time I'm going to ask you. If I don't get some straight answers I shall walk out of the door, call off the guards and take a statement from Maire against you.'

Jockey groaned, his hand going to his head.

Carney was prepared to wait all day. He unbuttoned his jacket to let some cool air circulate.

'We had an arrangement,' Jockey said, his head averted. 'She moved in with me. Every now and then she'd entertain some of my friends. I'd give her the dope, no charge. It suited all of us.'

Carney controlled himself, remembering what it was he was there for, willing himself to stay detached.

'I don't know what happened after the shooting. Didn't she tell you?'

'Drug pushing, pimping . . .' Carney shook his head in despair. 'We ought to lock you away in a zoo with the rest of the animals, only they'd probably complain about the smell. God knows what else will come out of this. You do realise you'll have to tell me what you know about the Raffertys before we discuss the deal?'

'No problem,' Jockey said. 'I'll tell you all you want to know. To get me to go into court and testify against them, the money will have to be safe in an overseas account, the tickets will have to be deposited with my solicitor, along with a new name and a new passport.'

Carney wondered if the plan came from some novel or whether the weedy looking individual lying in the bed was not as stupid as he looked. 'Let's hear it then,' he said, reaching for his notebook.

CHAPTER TWENTY ONE

Dublin, Tuesday June 12th

'Sorry I didn't phone you last night,' Walsh said. 'I spoke to the Commissioner.'

Carney took a chair and sat at the desk. 'Did he go for it?'

'Reluctantly. Although he did like the idea of nailing Rafferty. He's still worried about the risk. We're going to have thirteen men putting their lives on the line.'

'I know, but you have to balance it against the possible gains. If we do get hit, we have a chance of getting Rafferty on a serious charge. Attempted murder, conspiracy at the least. And we also have our "mole". I can't work a department without total trust in my men. If nothing comes out of it, we still have Jockey in reserve.'

'Are you going to tell me who you suspect of passing information to Rafferty?'

'I don't think it's fair at this stage. The only people who know this is a decoy run are you, me and the Commissioner. The escort has been told the general nature of the assignment but none of the details. They're all from outside the department. There's just one man who thinks it's for real.'

'What if they don't make a hit?'

'We can only assume that they either thought it too risky or the "mole" is someone I haven't even considered. Unless you want to consider the possibility that yourself or the Commissioner . . .'

Walsh raised his eyebrows. 'Have you discussed the operation with the escort?'

'I set it up yesterday in case the Commissioner gave the go ahead.'

He fished in his pocket and took out a rough sketch of the hospital grounds. 'They might strike at the hospital itself. We intend to take the stretcher out by the back entrance. The ambulance will be waiting at the steps. Two Gardai will act as attendants. I've borrowed uniforms for them. The two escort cars will be stationed at these points. One in the alleyway leading to the main entrance and the other by the main gates. The high wall running along here blocks out a view of the rear exit and the new wing cuts off any side access. We'll scatter men all round the building, keeping an eye on the reception area and the upper floors.'

'You think they might try at the hospital?'

'Because of the cover we have, I'd say not. Although we are at our most vulnerable. Everything static. The obvious route is to take the inland road. It's direct but there are traffic problems, even at that time in the morning. It would cause as much problem for them as it would for us. The coast road is quieter but takes longer and the roads are narrow in places. I don't think they'll try in the city at all. There are two bad spots nearer the Home. One is in the grounds itself. Along this avenue of trees.'

Carney opened out a sketch of the rambling estate. 'The Home was purchased three years ago. It used to be a country house. The owner died and his children put it up for sale. It stands in eight acres, most of it wooded. The front entrance is near the road so it isn't too bad, but the trees would be an ideal spot to hide.'

'Are you going to put men in the grounds?'

'Yes. But not in the trees. We don't want to scare them off. I thought we could put two men on each corner of the building. High profile at the front, hidden at the back.'

'So if they try from the back . . . ?'

'We'll have firepower outside the vehicles.'

'And the other spot?'

'Just here,' Carney replied, holding his finger on the map. 'The road winds down towards the sea then doubles back up a hill, almost a hairpin. We have to slow right down. On this side of the road is a stone wall about six feet high. On the other side there's a hill leading to a small wood.'

'They could try from the wood. How far is it to the road?'

'From the top of the hill . . . fifty or sixty yards.'

'Sniper?'

'Possibly, but it's risky. If they want to make sure of the job they'll have to get closer. They won't be able to see into the ambulance, so they don't know exactly where the stretcher would be lying.'

'What difference does it make how close they are? They could simply blast it from within range.'

'I don't think they could risk single shots. They would have to be close and use automatic fire, or very close to use something more powerful.'

'What, for God's sake?'

'I don't know but they have to destroy the ambulance to be certain they get Jockey.'

'Where would Rafferty get firepower like that?'

'I doubt he'll have his men turn up armed with rocket launchers. Something explosive and hand delivered would do.'

'I assume you have a theory?'

'This is the likely place. On the bend itself. On the other side of the wall, there's a drop. They can't use the wall as cover. If they are using explosives they can't use the hill. So it has to come from the road. The best way to handle it is to approach from beyond the Home. If they tail us we'd spot them.'

'Seems logical.'

'They have to halt the escort. If they knock out the lead car the ambulance is stuck. They could toss the explosives and be round the bend in the road in seconds. It would take time for the cars to turn and follow.'

'And you have a plan to stop them?'

'I intend to stop them before they have a chance to hit. Look at this.' On the reverse side of the sketch was a drawing of the hill in profile, the road clearly marked. 'From this position you can see almost a hundred yards up the road. I want a man here with binoculars and a radio. If they mean to get us on the bend they must be in line of sight from the hill before we get to it. The man with the radio can pass the word. We'd be ready for them.'

Walsh blew circles with the smoke from his cigar. 'Do you need anything from me?'

Carney shook his head and picked up the papers. 'No. It's all arranged. I was just waiting for the word.'

Co. Louth, Tuesday June 12th

Martin Graves cupped his hands and blew on them, massaging his fingers to ease the frozen ache in his bones. The semi-derelict house sat in a gully where a sloping field met the forest on the southern side of the border. It was not the ideal spot for storing the arms but the best they could manage. The safe houses along that part of the border were IRA controlled and Crowe could not risk contacting the owners. The word would get back within hours and his ex-colleagues would move to stop him.

A narrow lane ran up from the main road, weeds and grass from the hedgerow overgrowing the ruts made long ago by farm vehicles. Martin had been at the desolate spot for two nights and had not seen another soul. Occasionally a shot rang out in the distance as a neighbouring farmer took a pot at a pigeon or a rabbit, but otherwise he was cut off from the rest of the community. To keep him company, he had a small transistor radio and a stack of magazines borrowed from his married sister.

At twenty-two, with little formal education, he had joined the Provos, operating in west Belfast. It was there he had met Crowe. The next year had been eventful and he finally ended up in a hideout in Dundalk, nursing Crowe after an abortive attack on an RUC patrol. As Crowe developed his own ideas and strategy, leaving the Provos and INLA behind, Martin followed him, for no other reason than he did not know what else to do.

Now Crowe was back, recruiting members of his old unit. They had given Martin the task of guarding the weapons and he felt important again.

Martin was a small man, with thick brown hair and a tiny scar running across his top lip. The wound had been made by a sliver of wood, chipped out of a tree by a British Army bullet the day Crowe had been shot in the leg. He was proud of the way he had handled himself that day, applying a tourniquet to Crowe's leg and finding a doctor to tend the wound. He heard later that Crowe had fled the country and, with no one to follow, Martin had returned to live with his sister and her husband in Tullydonnell.

The renewed call had filled him with the old excitement and he accepted it without a second thought. His sister greeted his departure stoically. She gave him a watch and the magazines and waved goodbye from the door of the house.

The watch had stopped on the first day and he relied on the radio to check the time. He used it sparingly, afraid that the batteries might run low. It was his only contact with the outside world and was essential for the work he was to do on Thursday morning.

The arms were stored beneath the floorboards, laid out in rows. By six o'clock they were to be above ground, waiting for the lorry to collect them.

Portmarnock, Tuesday June 12th

Two concrete pillars marked the entrance to the Beechmount Nursing Home, the name etched on each one, the grooves painted in gold. A tarmac driveway led from the road in a sweeping curve up to the impressive mahogany double doors. Doric style pillars supported a balcony on the first floor.

The area in front of the building was marked out as a car park, the first three places bearing the names of senior staff in painted letters. At the back, a lawn ran down to a small stream, forming a natural boundary. The flower beds were dotted with marble statues and a line of shrubs gave privacy to the offices on the ground floor.

Boyle avoided the entrance, climbing over the wall and squeezing between the shrubs and a low wire fence. He padded over the lawn, crouching low. The front of the Nursing Home was in darkness, but the windows at the side were brightly lit. Boyle could make out the figure of a white coated nurse sitting behind a desk, a pair of glasses perched on the end of her nose as she studied something below the level of the window ledge.

He made his way down the drive. The entrance from the main road was almost a right angled turn, barely a car's width. Anyone wishing to enter the premises would have to slow to a crawl to make the turn safely.

A few yards from the turn, the road bent sharply to the right. Boyle paced the distance to the bend and then retraced his steps, standing at the kerb to view the approach from the other direction. As the wind off the sea ruffled his hair, the outline of a plan began to take shape.

A plan that had to work, he decided. That morning Brendan Rafferty had sent word through Callaghan that he wanted to see him. He was willing to take him on again. Boyle knew it had something to do with the brother. Sean had talked him into it. Whatever the reasons for it, Boyle was pleased to be a part of the set up again. He would prove he was capable, by organising and carrying through a job as important as this.

The Raffertys had somehow discovered that Jockey was to be moved to this place. Make sure he never gets there, they had told him.

Boyle smiled. Jockey was as good as dead already.

CHAPTER TWENTY TWO

Aughrim, Wednesday June 13th
Behan was first to waken, a draught from the ill-fitting door playing on his neck. His hand went to the spot to massage the ache. The sun shone weakly through the grimy windows and he turned over to escape the light.

Crowe was completely hidden by a pile of tangled sheets and, from the general state of the bed, Behan guessed he had a rough night. Behan decided it might be the only opportunity he had to slip out for a few hours. Swinging his legs off the bed, his toes came into contact with the cold floor and he cursed. Wrapping a sheet around him, he stepped gingerly to the sink, running the water until it was clear.

Ten minutes later he felt more human. The stubble had gone from his chin and the cold water had revived him sufficiently for him to realise he was hungry.

The remains of the sheep were still scattered about the kitchen and he gathered them together, jamming them into a plastic bag which he carried outside and threw in the ditch. The dew was thick on the ground and clear skies over the coast promised a fine day once the sun had penetrated the mist on the hills.

Returning to the house, he dressed, sighing with relief as he pulled thick woollen socks over his frozen feet. Crowe stirred, an arm appearing above the knotted sheets, grunts and groans audible beneath the tangle of clothes. Behan was about to slip through the door when Crowe sat up.

'Thank God we'll soon be away from here,' Crowe said. 'Where are you going?'

'Thought I'd go for a walk up the mountain.'

Behan's spirits sank as Crowe leapt from the bed. 'Wait and we'll walk together.'

They closed the door firmly behind them, Crowe with a rifle in the crook of his arm. The gentle slope at the base of the hill led to the crumbling stone wall and the steeper incline beyond. A rough path marked the route taken by the sheep to the lush grass at the top of the mountain.

Crowe climbed ahead of Behan. He looked back from time to time and waited for his colleague to catch up. At the top, where the mountain flattened into a plateau, they stopped to rest, their chests heaving with the effort of the climb.

'We have unfinished business here,' Crowe said.

Behan was puzzled. 'What else is there to do?'

Crowe snatched at a blade of grass, examining the stalk before placing it in his mouth. 'Pat Hume'.

'Pat's dead. The Rafferty mob killed him.'

Crowe raised his rifle, pointing it at the valley below. 'He was worth ten of them.'

'We're leaving tonight, we have to be at the border – '

'Wrong. We're not leaving until the score is settled.'

Behan swallowed hard. 'How – ?'

'It simply means that we operate with one unit short. It's not important. What is important is that Pat's death is avenged.'

'There's plenty of time after – '

'We're going to be too busy after tomorrow. The time to strike is now. You and me are going to pay a call on the Raffertys and teach them the price of a freedom fighter's life.'

Behan stood up. 'It's risky.'

'Just the opposite. No risk at all. They won't be expecting it.'

'It means we have to stay here.'

'Does that bother you?'

'It's a diversion we could do without.'

Crowe pulled the trigger. The metallic click made Behan jump. 'Don't worry. You'll get your chance. In the meantime, why don't you go and make us something to eat?'

Crowe watched as Behan descended the hill. He held the rifle to his shoulder, keeping the retreating figure in the centre of the cross-hairs on the telescopic sight. The plan could operate effectively with a unit short. They would function in pairs, each with a

Kalashnikov rifle and a rocket launcher. The targets had been chosen carefully. Each team would pick up their arms at the house near the border, leaving the area by different routes, entering the North by unmarked roads. They would proceed to pre-arranged locations, short of their target, and continue on foot across the countryside. Each unit had studied the lie of the land and had selected a spot that gave relative safety, combined with a clear view of the buildings being used by the voters at the elections. The police on duty would be the first target, taken out with single shots. The rockets would then be fired, followed by sustained rounds directed at the general public. In less than a minute they could kill a dozen people. If the rockets were on target, many more could die.

It would raise the campaign of terror to a new level. Beyond the game played by the Provos. Killing British soldiers was a game. Killing the police was a game. Killing people indiscriminately was terror. The idea of mounting a terrorist campaign was to strike fear in the hearts of ordinary men and women. A policeman or a soldier dead brought condemnation and a feeling that the game was being played to the rules. Legitimate targets in the war. What was needed was escalation to a level where everyone participated. *That* was real terror. *That* brought pressure on governments.

The new game would begin in Crossmaglen, in Newtownhamilton, in Keady and Killylea. With Crowe's absence, Newry would be spared. It made little difference to the overall plan. Thirty to fifty dead would do for a start.

The arms would be dumped after the attack to minimise chances of detection during escape. This campaign would be meticulously carried out. The initial consignment of arms could keep them in business for a year at least. They would strike haphazardly, mounting their attacks at random towns and villages throughout the North. Anything that moved would constitute a legitimate target. Any age, any sex, and any religion would do. It would pull men and resources away from towns, cause panic in London, create publicity worldwide and establish Crowe as Ireland's new Messiah.

Crowe shivered in anticipation. He shouldered the rifle and headed for the farmhouse.

CHAPTER TWENTY THREE

Co. Louth, Thursday June 14th

Martin Graves was dreaming of the time when he wandered the lanes around his home collecting birds' eggs. The sun was high in the sky and the air was full of the smell of new-mown hay. He wore an old jacket of his father's, a silver pin threaded through the lapel. His father had taught him how to blow the eggs. It had taken Martin months to perfect the art but once mastered he had never forgotten. His collection was housed in an old shoe box at the back of the wood shed and on rainy days he would go there, happy to spend the hours gazing at the fragile shells.

He was dreaming of such a moment when his neck began to itch. Half asleep, he brushed his hand over the offending spot. Awakening with a start he caught sight of an earwig as it dashed beneath his makeshift blanket. His nerves settled and the memory of where he was and what he was supposed to do came to him. He fumbled for the radio and switched it on, impatient for the music to end. Kicking the blanket to the far wall, he started to collect the odds and ends that had served him during his vigil.

The morning air held a chill, the sun struggling to penetrate the low clouds hanging above the forest. The early birds were about, circling the fields, calling to each other in their search for food.

Holding the radio to his ear, he grimaced as he realised there was less than an hour before the lorry was due to arrive.

By the time the weapons were lying over the ground floor of the house, the sweat was pouring down his face and his breath came in ragged gulps. Walking to the window, he peered down the lane. A mist rolled from the hill, obscuring the main road. Martin leaned against the wall, listening to his heart pounding in his chest. Another ten minutes and he would be free of the responsibility.

Dublin, Thursday June 14th

The alarm was partially muffled by the empty pillow case. Carney leaned over the edge of the bed to shut off the noise. He lay on his back for a moment, listening to see if anyone had been disturbed. His wife made a few groaning sounds, then settled again. Swinging his legs over the edge of the bed, he held the sheets clear of his body to avoid dragging them with him.

Downstairs, he stepped over the dog lying by the kitchen door and made for the household medicines in the corner cabinet. His sleep had been interrupted by half remembered dreams full of vague menace, and a dull ache over his left temple confirmed the less than perfect rest.

The coffee woke his system and he began to relax and view the day objectively. One part of him relished the chance of some action while another dreaded the responsibility. Most of his work was routine, a well disciplined chain of steps that were proven. Today was something different, the element of chance combined with danger. If his wife knew what was about to happen, she would be horrified.

He slipped out of the house quietly. The street was deserted, the milk bottles on the doorsteps evidence that the world was not yet awake. The car started with a faltering growl and he used the choke until he was on the main road and able to accelerate. As he drove, he went over the plan once again.

The ambulance was to be at the back entrance of the hospital at six o'clock. The stretcher with the decoy detective would be brought from the top floor, carried by two Gardai in hospital uniform. Carney and a Garda driver would make up the contingent in the ambulance. Behind them, he had seconded three of the crack shots from the Special Branch and the lead car would carry four heavily armed officers from the depot. The guard on Jockey's room had been doubled for the duration of the exercise.

They had tried to cover all aspects and Carney knew it was too late to make any changes. He was thankful that nothing new entered his head as he drove along the silent streets.

Boyle stretched, his arms at right angles to the bed. The cheap alarm clock showed the time as five thirty and he sank back into the pillow. A hazy glow filtered in through the flimsy curtains, heralding what was expected to be a sunny day. The prospect was not at all attractive to Boyle. For work of this nature he preferred dark mornings, with plenty of rain to cut down the number of potential witnesses.

The plan was his own, the Rafferty men taking orders from him. With this thought in his head, he reached over and took a cigarette from a packet on the bedside table. There were times, he thought, when the hardship of the early days seemed worthwhile. At last he had an opportunity to break into the inner circle of one of the most powerful families in Dublin. He intended to take that opportunity.

The plan would work. There was no way the ambulance could escape once it reached the bend in the road. He would save the Raffertys' stupid necks and he would have one of the largest networks of organised crime at his beck and call. All the people who had slighted him in the past, all those who had rippled the waters of his pond would get their just rewards.

He allowed himself a few more minutes, revelling in the tortured expressions on the faces of his victims. Then he was off the bed and dressing quickly. Without shaving or bothering to eat, he ran out of the house. In the eerie light of early morning he drove, window wide open, his red hair streaming behind him, the radio blaring out rock music from the twin speakers.

At five fifty, he picked up three of Rafferty's men. By six o'clock they had joined the other car less than a mile from the Nursing Home.

The transfer of the stretcher to the ambulance was carried out in silence, the white coated Gardai manhandling it down the steps at the rear of the main building.

Carney stood at the open doors, stepping aside to let them past, his eyes scanning the empty back streets and the surrounding rooftops for signs of movement. An unmarked car, parked unobtrusively amongst the official hospital vehicles, protected the side of the building leading to the main car park at the front. The occupants were crouched low in their seats, each watching a different part of the alleyway.

As the stretcher was loaded, Carney climbed into the back and checked that the radio was working. All units responded and he placed it on the bench at the back of the doors.

At Carney's signal, the driver pulled away. The lead car eased forward, the engine purring quietly as the special tyres crunched over the loose stones. The rear escort joined them at the main entrance, quickly closing the gap. With sirens blaring, they sped along the road, jumping the red lights. On the outskirts of the city, the sirens were switched off and the pace settled to a steady forty miles per hour.

Carney picked up the radio as they neared their destination, his thumb hovering over the call button. Shivers ran up and down his spine as the built-up area fell behind. He could feel the tension growing as the coast came into view and the ambulance slowed on the winding road. The familiar scenery suddenly seemed alien and unfriendly, every twist in the road, every overhang of trees, part of the menace all around. He took a deep breath and checked with the cars in front and rear, feeling easier at the sound of reassuring voices.

Co. Louth, Thursday June 14th

Graves clenched his hands into tight balls to stop them shaking. It was six thirty and the sun was climbing higher, illuminating the corners of the field. The mist had lifted and he could see the road at the end of the lane. Birds twittered in the hedges and he thought he heard the steady drone of a tractor somewhere in the distance.

He kept the radio to his ear, growing more nervous as the disc jockey gave the five-minute time checks. He had worked with the group in the past and it was not like them to be late.

At six forty-five he started to pace the cobbled yard at the front of the house. The fluttering in his stomach was turning to a nagging ache and his heart was beginning to race. It had never occurred to him that there might be a hitch, had never crossed his mind that he might be required to use some initiative. They had left him without transport. It was over five miles to the nearest village and he would be seen if he ventured onto the roads. Relief flooded over him at the sound of the heavy engine. Switching off the radio, he dashed into the house and dragged some of the arms nearer to the door. The noise grew louder and he heard the driver changing gear.

As the vehicle turned up the lane he paused in his efforts, wiping his forehead with the sleeve of his jacket. Voices called from the yard outside, indistinct at first. He moved to the door and opened it wide. His eye caught a movement in the shadows as someone ran to the back of the house.

They were on him in seconds. The chattering rotors of a helicopter sounded somewhere to his left and he saw the familiar outline sweep in low over the trees. His arms were pinned to the wall. Heavy boots kicked his ankles, spreading his legs. A hand grasped the back of his neck, pushing his face against rough stone. He felt his clothes being pulled from his back and voices were calling instructions. Men poured past him into the house.

His mind went blank as they frogmarched him down the lane. He was half pushed, half carried over the hedge, his head bent as the rotor blades slashed the air. Arms lifted him upwards and he saw the ground falling away.

Soon the house was a dot beneath him and he found it difficult to believe that moments before he had stood within its crumbling walls. No one spoke as the machine rattled and vibrated through the base of the white fluffy clouds. The men in uniform stared at him. He knew there was nothing he could say.

CHAPTER TWENTY FOUR

Portmarnock, Thursday June 14th
The Garda on the hill yawned, sucking in lungfuls of air. The long grass was damp and he could feel water in the bottom of his shoes. A thin mist swept in from the sea and he constantly cleaned the lens of the ten-by-fifty binoculars dangling at his neck. He scanned the road ahead, picking out a solitary blue van as it made its way towards him. He activated the radio and informed Carney.

'We're about five minutes away,' the Inspector advised him. 'Keep the channel open. I'll give you a countdown every sixty seconds from now on.'

He acknowledged the instructions and put the radio within easy reach on the grass. The van approached the bend, slowing to a crawl as the driver braked hard. The Garda tensed, training the glasses on the cab. The van negotiated the bend, accelerating away towards Dublin and he breathed a sigh of relief.

'Four minutes!'

'Okay. Four minutes. The road is clear so far.'

Swirling mist cut his visibility for a moment, clearing as a fresh gust of wind came in from the sea. He thought of warning Carney about the unpredictable view, then changed his mind. The Inspector was too far on to alter things now. A man and his dog appeared on the far side of the road. The man was wearing a loose-fitting raincoat that flapped in the wind. The Garda watched him for a few seconds, deciding that the raincoat was being blown about too much to be hiding anything heavy.

'Three minutes!'

'All clear.'

As he switched the radio to reception, a car headed up the road in the direction of the Home. The angle was bad for him to see clearly but he thought there were at least three men.

'You have a car in front of you, travelling slowly.'

'Can you make it out?'

'Green . . . Renault Eleven . . . three men, possibly more . . .'

'Two minutes . . . perhaps a bit less.'

'It's slowing. It's stopped at the bend.'

He swung the binoculars to the top of the road and his heart skipped a beat. 'You have a car approaching as well. Too far away to make out. Blue . . .'

'About sixty seconds!'

The Garda wiped a trickle of sweat from his brow. The binoculars suddenly felt very heavy and he was unsure of which car to watch.

'Thirty seconds . . . we can see the tops of the trees . . .'

'You have a car at the bend and another approaching.'

'We can see the car now. We're about two hundred yards from the bend.'

As Carney spoke the car moved off, taking the bend quickly. The Garda refocussed the glasses and caught the flashes of light. 'He's flashing his headlights at the approaching car . . . three flashes in return. The car ahead of you is doing a u-turn. Twenty yards from the corner . . .'

'We're slowing down.'

The Garda stole a glance over his shoulder, in time to see the ambulance pull over to the kerb. The rear car accelerated and the two escorts continued alone. 'They're waiting on the bend. One at the kerb, the other out in the road.'

The rear escort swung sideways across the road, blocking it completely. The lead car crept forward, keeping well to the side as the driver inched it round the sharp curve. As the Garda car came into sight, the Renault lurched forward, the tyres spinning on the wet tarmac.

'They're moving . . .'

The Garda car came to an abrupt halt and men piled out, their weapons raised.

From his vantage point on the hill, the Garda had a clear view of the whole scene. He heard commands being shouted and voices yelling in return. A rattle of gunfire sent the birds streaming from their nests.

The driver of the Renault was trying to turn, his off front wheel deflated. A rear door opened and a man jumped out, his arm raised above his head, something heavy in the palm of his hand. In one quick motion his hands came together and he leaned back about to throw the object. A burst of gunfire echoed through the hills and the man fell, the object falling into the vehicle through the open door. A blinding flash caused the Garda to drop the glasses. A roar rent the air as the grenade went off. A split second later the petrol tank erupted, sending an orange ball of flame skywards. The Gardai on the road were thrown backwards by the blast.

'What the hell's going on?' Carney screamed down the radio.

The Garda failed to hear him. He was on his feet, running to the brow of the hill, the binoculars held to his eyes as the blue car roared off in the direction it had come. The road was blocked, the debris of the wrecked car belching out thick clouds of black smoke. The Garda watched until the retreating vehicle was out of sight. He panted as he jogged back to the radio. 'He's away,' he said. 'We can't get through.'

Carney sprinted from the ambulance, two white coated Gardai at his heels. Racing round the bend, they came to an abrupt halt as the heat from the flames blasted their faces. Several Gardai were crawling away from the inferno, their faces blackened.

Carney approached the blazing car cautiously, his arm held across his face. The wind blew the smoke over the road and up the hill towards the officer with the binoculars.

Carney met him at the stone wall. 'Have you alerted traffic?' Carney asked, above the roar of the flames.

The Garda nodded. Carney turned to inspect the road. The blazing car had spewed debris over the whole surface, blocking it completely. 'Is everyone okay?' he shouted.

One of the white coated Gardai came towards him. 'They're a bit shaken, nothing serious.'

'Get onto headquarters,' Carney said. 'Tell them what happened and get them to clear up this mess.'

The officer jogged to the ambulance and Carney followed. He would nail Daly's balls to the desk, he thought grimly, as the driver reversed down the hill. At the bottom of the incline the ambulance swung round, heading back to Dublin.

Dublin, Thursday June 14th

Boyle parked the car in a side street. Sweat trickled down his face and he could not think straight. It had all happened so quickly. The burst of gunfire had taken him by surprise and he could only sit and watch. When the car exploded he had panicked and fled the scene. Now he was in real trouble. The survivors would report back to Rafferty and he would be seen to have failed again. His dreams of glory had been shattered in a few brief seconds. Rafferty would now be his enemy, not his benefactor.

As he sat in the car, his body began to shake uncontrollably. Anger welled up, turning his face scarlet. A vein pulsed in the side of his head and he thumped the steering wheel in frustration. All he could think of was Carney and his hatred for Carney. He had to act and act quickly if he was to save his reputation, if he was to take his revenge.

Carney had a family, he thought. Two children. One of them a young girl. Breathing heavily, he forced himself to be calm. There was still a chance.

As he regained control, he was convinced he could salvage something. He would need to think out the details more clearly. That was all that was needed. No need to hurry it. Feeling much better, he abandoned the car and walked towards the main road, a new spring in his step.

Martin Crowe stood by the window of the small flat and looked out on the dingy street. Dustbins littered the alleyway, piled high with leftover food and empty containers. The local cats were out in force, sniffing the decaying refuse, their heads constantly turning as they watched for danger.

Crowe hated big cities. Despite the outward security and anonymity that crowded streets provided, he felt uncomfortable and claustrophobic.

Behan had been gone too long. Crowe had sent him for food more than an hour ago.

A cheap plastic radio sat on a table in the centre of the room. In the corner, a black and white television showed cartoon characters beneath a layer of shimmering silver dots. Crowe was beginning to feel irritable. The strikes in the North should have filtered through to the newsrooms by now.

The sparsely furnished, top-floor flat was grubby even by his standards. He had taken it on a short lease, no questions asked. It had one decrepit chair, a bed and a couch that was a threadbare skeleton of its former self.

A noise on the stairs brought him to his feet. Behan knocked as they had arranged. Two short raps followed by a heavy one. Straightening his leg, he held it stiff, limping painfully to the door.

'What kept you?'

'It took me ages to find a supermarket,' Behan explained, dropping a brown paper bag on the chair.

Crowe pushed past, taking items from the bag. 'I told you not to buy anything that needed cooking.'

Behan looked at the tin. 'They're already cooked. We'll have to eat them cold.'

Crowe tossed the beans to one side. 'Did you bring the tablets?'

Behan reached in his pocket and threw a box which Crowe caught. Crowe tore the lid off and swallowed four of the white tablets in one gulp.

'Anything on the radio?'

Crowe screwed up his face as the bitter tasting medicine made him shudder. He ignored the question, standing in front of the television, his legs apart, his hands clenched at his side.

'There should have been something by now,' said Behan.

'I know that, you fucking idiot.'

Behan stepped back, shaken by the intensity of the reply. Crowe was visibly trembling.

The news bulletin came on the hour. A bland mixture of the international and local events. Crowe snatched up the telephone and listened to the purring sound.

'They should have finished by now,' he said. 'They should all be back at their bases.'

'Maybe . . .'

'Maybe, maybe,' sneered Crowe. 'They were supposed to phone. Each unit was to call this number . . .'

Behan stood up and edged towards the door. Crowe was prowling, his eyes bulging, his arms waving frantically. Behan had studied Crowe in many situations, but he had never seen him react like this. Crowe suddenly rounded on the television, lashing out with his foot. There was a loud crack as the tube imploded and sparks jumped from the tangle of wires.

'Those bastards,' Crowe screamed. 'Those lousy bastards.'

Behan stood with his shoulders slumped, wondering how much longer he could survive.

CHAPTER TWENTY FIVE

Dublin, Friday June 15th

Walsh ushered Carney into his office, waving away the secretary who was fussing with the papers on his desk.

'Where is he?' Carney asked.

Walsh opened a drawer and pulled out his pipe. He sucked noisily as he held the match to it. When he was satisfied that the tobacco was glowing nicely, he looked at the Inspector through a haze of blue smoke. 'We'll take care of it,' he said. 'You have enough problems on your plate.'

Carney tapped his fingers on the edge of the desk, trying to keep calm. 'Why didn't you consult me first?'

'Don't take it personally. You did a good job. Let's leave it at that.'

'How did you know?'

'It wasn't hard to work out. I checked with Byrne. He didn't know anything about the dummy run. Fitzgerald didn't know anything. Only Daly let on that he knew what was afoot. Said he overheard you talking to Byrne. It wasn't hard to work out that if Byrne didn't know, then Daly must have been the one you were setting up.'

'Why did you have to know?'

'In case the plan worked.'

Carney shook his head. 'What difference did it make?'

'I thought you might not handle the situation delicately. Look, Daly is not going to admit it.'

'Have you asked him?'

'Yes.'

'Jesus Christ!'

'There's no way we can prove it unless Brendan Rafferty volunteers us the information. And he isn't going to do that. If

Daly keeps tight-lipped we're out on a limb. He couldn't continue to work with you in the department now that the trust is broken and we can't kick him off the force without any proof.'

'So what have you done?'

'I transferred him to Cork.'

'You did what?'

'I had a word with an old friend of mine. Gave him enough of the facts for him to draw his own conclusions and sent him Daly. I don't think Daly will ever be in a position to do any harm.'

'I don't believe it.'

'What would you have done? Beaten it out of him?'

Carney sighed. 'Where is he now?'

Walsh tapped the bowl of his pipe against the rim of a waste-paper basket at his feet. 'He's on . . . vacation. Forget it, Pat. You concentrate on Jockey. Get the information you need. The Commissioner signed the papers this morning. By the way,' Walsh called as Carney was leaving, 'I see you've put in for a vacation yourself. Going anywhere special?'

'Spain.'

'I hope it's not a working holiday.'

Molly Adams changed her grip on the canvas bag to ease the ache in the palm of her hand. This morning the bag was heavier than usual on account of her husband's bonus from the building site. It never amounted to much, but enough to buy a few extra groceries from the corner shop.

She realised she had made a mistake. She should have collected the groceries on the way back from her visit to the city. Then she would have saved herself the trouble of lugging them around the streets. She made the run into the centre of Dublin once a week to see her mother in the Home. It had been going on for years. Too long, she thought grimly as she struggled along.

The bus stop came into view as she rounded the corner. Soon she could rest her limbs. The journey took twenty minutes, plenty of time for her to recover.

She enjoyed the outing and looked forward to seeing the children who caught the same bus to the local school. If she was lucky, she might see the handsome young man in the pinstripe suit who carried a leather briefcase with initials imprinted in gold lettering on either side of the handle.

The blond-haired girl was at the stop, leaning against the wall, her bag dangling from a long strap on her shoulder. The twins were there, identical in their matching hairstyles and uniforms. She smiled and nodded, setting her bag down. The blond-haired girl acknowledged and said, 'Good morning'. Molly glanced down the road for signs of the bus and checked the time on her watch. Despite the heavier load, she was earlier than usual.

The girl appeared from the side street, long hair falling over her shoulders, a satchel weighted down with books swinging from her hand. Molly recognised her immediately, thinking that the full complement of children was now assembled.

Afterward, she found it difficult to remember whether it was the scream or the flash of white sock that attracted her attention. What she did remember was that one minute the girl was walking towards her and the next she was gone. The car that accelerated away from the kerb at the same moment was lost in the traffic before she could react.

Celbridge, Friday June 15th

Boyle parked the car at the rear of the house. The building sat at the back of two large oak trees, obscured from the road. A dry stone wall surrounded the grounds, marking out some long-forgotten boundary line. The house had been in the Boyle family for as long as he could remember. Apart from a brief and acrimonious occupation by his sister three years before, none of the others had shown any interest in it. The inside walls upstairs were damp and overgrown with a bluish mould where the rain had seeped in through the cracked slates. The old wallpaper was stained and peeling.

Several floorboards were missing on the stair landing and Boyle deftly avoided them, the unconscious girl dangling from his arms. He chose the bedroom at the back of the house, partly because it seemed the obvious thing to do and partly because the windows in this section of the house were so encrusted in a dark, greasy film, they were safe from prying eyes.

The girl fell easily onto the bed, murmuring as she bounced on the mattress. The bed was a relic from the 1920s, with an iron frame supporting a base of rusty springs. Taking two nylon ropes from the floor, he secured the girl's legs to the two posts at the foot of the bed and then fastened her arms to the posts at the head. Raising her eyelids, he satisfied himself that she was well enough drugged to be left alone. He closed the bedroom door and locked it. Driving slowly, he made for Lucan and the nearest telephone.

Dublin, Friday June 15th

Mary Carney felt like screaming. The carpet sweeper was leaving more on the carpet than it was picking up and she hated the job of emptying it. The dog was following her around looking for attention, sticking its damp nose under her feet every time she paused for breath. She sat on the couch, her eyes closed. Coffee, she decided. That was the only answer. Shooing the dog away, she dragged herself to the kitchen and plugged in the kettle.

The dog barked in the hall as the postman dropped an envelope through the letter box. Coffee in hand, Mary stooped to pick the letter from the carpet, then dodged quickly into the living room, closing the door before the dog could follow.

The envelope contained the confirmation of their holiday booking. Six weeks, she thought, and then she would be lying on a golden beach beside a deep blue sea, with nothing to worry about except her exposure to the unaccustomed heat.

She sipped her drink, leafing through the papers, reading every clause. A wasp bumped into the window, distracting her for a moment. As she relaxed, she began to think about all the good things of summer. The longer days, the smell of flowers and, most of all, the change for the better in her own personality.

The telephone rang, interrupting her reverie. Reluctantly, she set the papers on the couch and wandered into the hall.

The dog jumped up and she brushed it away. 'Mrs Carney,' she said.

'Listen carefully,' the disembodied voice said. 'I have your daughter.'

CHAPTER TWENTY SIX

Dublin, Friday June 15th

'How is she?' Walsh asked as Carney joined him in the car.

'A lot calmer now. I think the drugs are working.'

'Is she happy with the officer?'

'Yes. She met Hilary at last year's dance. No problem there.'

'Robinson will meet us at your office. Fitzgerald insisted on staying on as well.'

'Fitzgerald should be asleep,' Carney said as Walsh started the engine.

'I thought it would be a good idea.'

Carney turned away, his mind in a turmoil. The journey to Harcourt Street proceeded in silence, Walsh thinking how he was going to meet the first part of the kidnappers' demands and hold Carney in check and Carney wondering how he could persuade Walsh to let him handle the case.

As they entered the building, Superintendent Robinson met them in the corridor.

'Do you know the Superintendent?' Walsh asked Carney.

The two men shook hands. They had never met but Carney had heard of him. He had handled the Gracewell case the year before when the son of one of Ireland's wealthiest families had been kidnapped in Cork. Once in Carney's office they closed the door, cancelled all incoming calls and stocked up on hot coffee.

Robinson smoothed back his thinning hair with both hands and then wiped them on a faded white handkerchief. 'We've just had the one call,' he said. 'An unidentified voice rang Mrs Carney at approximately ten minutes past nine this morning and informed her that he was holding your daughter. Your wife contacted you at this office immediately after the call. The school was checked and they confirmed your daughter did not attend today.' Carney nodded. 'You then called Superintendent Walsh and you both proceeded to your home.'

'Yes,' Walsh said.

'Now, I understand that your wife was extremely upset, but as far as she could remember, the gist of the message was as follows . . .'

Walsh offered them both sugar and Robinson paused before he continued.

'The voice said that your daughter had been kidnapped and was being held hostage for a man called Jockey, currently receiving treatment for drug addiction and gunshot wounds and who is co-operating with the Gardai in the matter of the activities of the Rafferty family.' He hesitated, clearing his throat. 'The only demand made was that the matter should be kept from the newspapers and television and that if one word was mentioned in the media your daughter would be killed.' Robinson flicked over a page in his notebook. 'We are to await a further phone call tomorrow morning.'

'That's it,' Carney said.

'Does your daughter always travel to school the same way?'

Carney shrugged. 'I think so. I'm always gone before she leaves the house, but as far as I know she catches the bus each morning just round the corner from the house.'

'First of all,' Robinson said, 'we're going to find out exactly where she was lifted.'

Brendan Rafferty stared at Charlie, his face a mask of utter disbelief. Gradually, his jaw began to move, then his bottom lip trembled and Charlie was reminded of Rafferty's father working up a rage. Instinctively he moved the chair back a few inches, his body tensed, waiting for the explosion.

'Boyle's kidnapped Carney's daughter?' Rafferty hissed, his knuckles turning white as they gripped the linen tablecloth.

Charlie nodded slowly. 'Yes,' he said, checking it over in his mind to make sure he had it entirely right. 'This morning.'

'And what were you doing, you fucking idiot?'

Charlie looked surprised. 'He said it was okay.'

'You mindless . . .' Rafferty collapsed backwards in his chair, his head rolling from side to side, a low moan coming from deep in his throat. It took him some time to recover his senses. Charlie sat passively, waiting for the storm to subside, nursing his hurt feelings.

'Tell me again,' Rafferty said, his voice calmer. 'Tell me exactly what happened.'

Charlie concentrated hard, trying to remember every detail. 'Boyle came to the pub last night. Said he had another plan to deal with Jockey. Said he had borrowed a car from one of Callaghan's men at the disco. He works for Callaghan a few nights a week . . .'

'Callaghan!' Rafferty interrupted, becoming agitated again. 'Go and get him. I don't care what he's doing or where he is, bring him to me.'

Charlie was relieved that he had been given something to do. He felt uncomfortable in the room with Rafferty. He had a vague sense that Rafferty thought it was his fault. Rafferty rose from the table and caught Charlie by the arm. 'Don't tell him what this is all about. Don't say a word.'

'What if he says he can't come?' Charlie asked, anxious not to do the wrong thing again.

'Use your initiative,' Rafferty told him, grabbing Charlie's left hand and forming it into a fist.

The light dawned and Charlie smiled, his eyes widening.

Carney felt surprisingly calm as he parked opposite the Rafferty house. Everything appeared normal. Rafferty's car was in the drive and he glimpsed Rose hanging washing on a line at the side of the house. 'Let's go,' he said to Fitzgerald. 'Let's find out what this evil bastard knows about it.'

'Yes?' Rose said, more as a challenge than a greeting. She stepped aside when they ignored her. 'You have a warrant?' she asked. They pushed open the front door of the house and walked in. She followed.

Brendan Rafferty was in the living room. He registered a brief moment of shock when Carney and Fitzgerald entered, but quickly regained his composure. 'It's alright, Rose,' he said, indicating that she should leave. 'We're old friends.' He dismissed the idea of challenging their illegal entry. It would serve no purpose and he was wary of Carney's reaction to any pressure.

'Must be nearly a year, Inspector,' he said. He sat down, stalling for time so that he could assess the situation. 'I thought you were desk-bound?' he said to Fitzgerald.

'It gets boring.'

'What can I do for you?'

Carney picked up a porcelain ballerina from the side table. 'If you didn't know and had a clear conscience you'd be on the phone to your solicitor by now.'

'You can set the statue down, Inspector. I'm no Callaghan. Why don't you just say what you came to say?'

Carney replaced the porcelain figure carefully and looked around the room. It was more or less as he remembered it. One or two of the paintings by the door seemed to be new additions, but otherwise everything appeared the same.

'My wife had a phone call this morning,' he said. 'Didn't recognise the voice, but the man said he was holding my daughter.'

Rafferty felt Fitzgerald's eyes studying him closely.

'You can imagine what effect that had on her. She's a good soul. Looks after the family well, minds her own business, does things for the Church. You can also imagine what effect seeing her hurt like that had on me.'

Rafferty nodded, swallowing hard.

'Then there's my daughter, of course. You'd like her. At that awkward stage when they like to be treated as children but know they no longer are. She was on her way to school apparently, when . . . terrible thing to do to a child. God knows what she must be going through. We never coddled her, you know. But still . . . it's hard to imagine the terror of it all on someone so young. The people who can do such a thing, well, it beggars description.'

Rafferty realised that the critical point was approaching fast. 'Believe me, Inspector,' he said, carefully measuring his words, 'I know how you feel. What can I do for you?'

'You can pick up the phone and call it all off now,' Carney said evenly. 'If I have her back this afternoon . . .'

'What makes you think I could do that?'

'Oh, it was just something the man said.'

'Something he said?'

'One of your pushers is willing to talk. My daughter is being held hostage to make sure he doesn't and if you tell me you don't know anything about it, you'll make me very angry. Very angry indeed.'

Rafferty carefully considered his options. Fitzgerald sat impassively to his left, drumming his fingers on the arm of the chair, a neutral expression on his face, his legs stretched out, the beginnings of a hole showing on the sole of his right shoe. Carney was simply waiting. He stood in the middle of the room, watching and waiting.

Rafferty breathed deeply, trying hard to remain composed. If he denied any involvement in the events of the morning, he risked an explosion of anger from Carney he felt he would be unable to control. If he told the truth, that one of his men had taken things into his own hands, he would be inextricably involved, the final nail in the lid of a coffin that threatened to close on him and his family forever.

He considered the possibility of a deal. Boyle's name might buy him some time and immunity from the kidnapping. At best it would turn matters back twenty-four hours, leaving him with the problem of Jockey. At worst it could provide additional evidence to a jury of the nature of his operations, tie him in to the abduction and give credence to the violent picture of the family that Jockey was bound to create.

Carney was prepared to wait all day for an answer. He knew that Rafferty had to be involved somehow, even if the kidnapping had not been authorised. For the first time in fifteen years he felt he had the upper hand. There was no feeling of triumph, just a sadness that almost overwhelmed him.

'Inspector Carney,' Rafferty said. 'Let me talk to my solicitor.'

Co. Armagh, Friday June 15th

They had taken him when the light was on, moving along the sides of the room, out of his line of vision. The straps holding his arms had been untied first, then the ones around his ankles. The head restraint was left in position until the last minute, giving them a chance to place a hood over his head. He thought there had been at least three of them. As they supported him on the walk to the door, he had sensed the movement of another man ahead of him, in addition to the two who held his arms.

The room Graves was now in was sparsely furnished. A table dominated the centre of the floor with two chairs opposite him. A bare light bulb dangled from a yellowing ceiling, held at the end of a frayed flex. The door to his left had no handle on the inside. A peephole was positioned about two feet from the top and what looked like a cat flap had been cut into the bottom, the trailing edge flush with the floor. The room was windowless.

Graves had difficulty in turning his head, the muscles in his neck stiff and sore from his efforts to avoid the harsh glare of the light. He was hungry and thirsty, his stomach rumbling, his tongue sticking to the roof of his mouth. He strained his ears, desperate to catch even the slightest sound from outside his prison to let him know he was not completely alone. All he heard was the rhythmic whisper of his own breathing.

Despite the ordeal and the damage to his nerves, the tense, panicky feeling was gradually subsiding to be replaced by an overwhelming desire to sleep. His search for a plausible story had given way to a kind of despair, an indifference that he felt might yet be his salvation.

As he dozed, he wondered idly what his sister was doing and whether or not she thought of him from time to time. He thought too of the men he was supposed to meet. Perhaps he had made a mistake or maybe some farmer had spotted him and called the Gardai.

The events of the day before seemed so far away, he was having difficulty believing that they really happened.

The cat flap opened with a jarring rattle, jerking him upright, his heart beating wildly. A white enamel bowl sat on the floor of his cell, wisps of steam floating into the air from the centre of the dish. He waited until his heartbeat settled and took deep breaths to compose himself. The smell tempted him out of his chair. Lifting the bowl carefully, he sniffed, balancing it in the palms of his hands. The thick soup lapped against the sides and he placed it quickly on the table. Holding the rim of the bowl firmly between the finger and thumb of each hand he raised it to his lips and started to sip.

His face contorted as he swallowed the first mouthful. The liquid trickling down his throat was saturated with salt.

CHAPTER TWENTY SEVEN

Dublin, Friday June 15th

Behan awoke to find Crowe sitting in the chair, his expressionless eyes staring at the far wall.

They had heard nothing from the units. No word that the attacks had taken place. The mangled remains of the television rested in a corner and the evening newspapers sat in a pile by the door. Behan slipped quietly from the bed and dressed in the shadows. He ran his fingers through the two days' growth of beard on his chin and wished it was all over. The strain of living with Crowe was beginning to tell. His nerves were shattered and he could not think straight.

Crowe ignored him as he pottered about the flat. He sat motionless in the chair, seemingly unaware of his surroundings.

An hour later, Behan put on his jacket, determined to get out of the flat so he could relax. As he was heading for the door, Crowe leapt from his seat, knocking him sideways. The door flew back, hitting the wall, clouds of pulverised plaster exploding outwards in a grey cloud. Behan hesitated, then decided to follow. He took the stairs three at a time in his effort to keep up with the limping man.

At the door, Behan caught sight of Crowe as he turned the corner, heading for the car. Behan ran across the alley, scattering the dustbins.

The car was hemmed in by other vehicles and Crowe vaulted the bonnet, falling into the road as he landed. Cars screeched to a halt, the drivers shouting abuse. Crowe struggled with the key, eventually opening the driver's door and leaping in. Behan banged on the window, trying to attract Crowe's attention. The car reversed, smashing into the one behind. A crowd gathered as Crowe crunched his way free. Amid the squeal of tyres and the sound of blaring horns, the car shot away from the kerb, the rear end swerving violently on the slippery surface.

Behan gazed in horror at the speeding vehicle. Backing away from the scene of havoc, he brushed through the group of onlookers.

Crowe had deserted him. It was his chance to escape.

John Boyd closed his briefcase and shook his head. 'My advice is say absolutely nothing. This wasn't your idea. You hardly know the man. Any admission, however tenuous, of your involvement with this man can be very damaging, not only in regard to the lifting of this girl, but at any other stage of enquiries.'

Rafferty made as if to speak, then thought better of it.

'If you admit to knowing this man it would give them the excuse to hold you. You don't really think you could give them his name and hear nothing more about it. They'd grill you till the cows came home.' Boyd rose from the chair. 'Do you want me to tell them?'

Rafferty nodded, casting an anxious glance at the door. Boyd walked over to it.

'Don't say a word,' he said, looking back.

Carney entered alone, leaving Fitzgerald to finish his coffee in the kitchen.

'Inspector Carney,' Boyd said, avoiding the policeman's steady gaze. 'My client called me to ask advice and I've talked the matter over. My client wishes to state that until your visit this afternoon and your illegal entry to these premises, he had no knowledge of the events of which you spoke, had no contact or discourse with the perpetrators of the act, and has no reason to believe he can help you.'

Carney adjusted his coat and turned the collar down. He slowly fastened the buttons, adjusting the twisted belt that hung at the back.

'Thank you, Mr Boyd,' he said. 'I think that in the circumstances you have not given Mr Rafferty sound advice. I wish to state that whatever the outcome, I intend to nail your client's balls to the wall, pickle them and serve them to my dog. You have my solemn assurance on that. In the meantime, I wish you both a very good day.'

Fitzgerald joined him in the hall. 'Any luck?' he asked, knowing from Carney's expression and his brief time in the room that things had not gone as planned.

'Thank you, Rose,' Carney called as he opened the door.

Rose put Fitzgerald's cup under the running tap, washing the remains of the black liquid down the sink. She half turned at the sound of her name. She watched as they closed the gate and walked over to their car, holding back the kitchen curtain to get an unobstructed view.

Boyd followed them out shortly afterwards, his shiny black shoes beating a tattoo on the concrete path.

The living room door opened and closed and she heard the heavy tread of Brendan's feet as he climbed the stairs.

Celbridge, Friday June 15th

Sinead half twisted her body, shaking her wrist until the watch slithered round into her line of vision. The light outside was still bright and the far wall was bathed in a golden glow.

The missing part of the day returned to her memory in disjointed pieces. She remembered leaving the house and kissing the dog at the gate. The schoolbag had been heavy and she had taken it off her shoulder and let it dangle from her hand. She remembered being just in time for the bus, but the next memory was of strange dreams. Someone had carried her up a flight of stairs and there were vague recollections of being tossed onto a bed.

Her eyes still felt heavy, a dull ache spreading over her temples as she fought to keep them open. She found it difficult to think in the warm room and she seemed unable to move freely. For all the strangeness of her situation, she was surprised how calm she felt. She should be worrying about the school, about her parents, but they surfaced only as facts, untainted by emotion.

Birds twittered close by, occasionally casting shadows in the room as they swooped from their perches over the house. She liked the sounds they made. Closing her eyes, she imagined herself in her bedroom at home, listening to the birds in her own garden. Minutes later she was asleep.

Dublin, Friday June 15th

The car skidded as it took the corner, the rear end straying over the broken white line in the middle of the road. Crowe fought to correct the slide as oncoming traffic swerved to avoid him. He gripped the wheel tightly, the muscles of his arms bulging with the strain. Counting the streets off the main road, he swung the car right at the fourth one down from the traffic lights.

The house gleamed in the afternoon sun, the black slates on the roof reflecting the rays in a splash of dazzling white. Crowe jumped from the car and opened the boot. Tearing the sacking from the rifle, he stepped onto the pavement, the barrel of the gun resting on the car roof.

Rose came out of the house and checked the washing on the line. She began pulling out the wooden pegs. The upstairs toilet flushed and she inclined her head to the back window.

The deafening noise sent her heart pounding. She dropped her basket, strewing the washing over the grass. Bits of wood and stone exploded all around and she felt a stinging sensation burn across her cheek. Above the noise, someone was screaming loudly. The next thing she knew, she was on the ground, crouched behind the dustbin as a hail of bullets whistled above her head.

Suddenly, the shooting stopped. A car engine over-revved and tyres screeched on the road outside. She heard Sean calling her name and as she crawled up the path she saw him dash from the front of the house towards her.

Brendan followed, his right shoulder covered in blood. He was shaking and his face was ashen. The path was littered with glass. All the windows had been blown in and jagged holes peppered the door.

A car pulled up at the gate and Callaghan stepped unsteadily to the pavement. 'God in heaven,' he said, catching Charlie by the arm. 'What the hell is going on?'

CHAPTER TWENTY EIGHT

Dublin, Saturday June 16th

Carney gave Mary's hand a squeeze and was pleased to see a flicker of a smile in return. Her leg trembled as she leaned forward on the edge of the couch, her eyes following Robinson round the room as he laid the network of wires in a neat line along the skirting board.

Robinson smiled in return. 'Nearly finished. We'll try not to make the house too untidy.' When he was satisfied that everything was in order he stood in the middle of the floor and explained the procedure. 'I know it looks a bit of a dog's dinner, but really, it's fairly simple. This is a tape recorder, nothing special. We've linked it to your telephone so that all incoming and outgoing conversations can be automatically recorded. You have nothing to do. As soon as the receiver is lifted, the recorder is activated.' To demonstrate, he lifted the phone to his ear, pausing so they could see the reels of the device in motion. 'When the receiver is replaced, it stops.' He replaced it with a click and the recorder switched itself off. 'In addition, these wires here are for the benefit of the telephone operators. They're standing by to try and trace the source of the call. You probably know how it works. Time is of the essence. I must warn you that the person calling will, no doubt, be aware that his call is subject to trace and will in all likelihood keep the message short. You know what to do?'

Mary bit her lip, nodding.

'I know it will be difficult, but try and keep calm. If you sound in control, the caller is more likely to be relaxed and more open to questions. Your request for proof that he has your daughter will be expected. Hopefully he will let her say a few words to you on the phone. I don't want you to be distressed if she sounds distraught. The man will have instructed her for the maximum effect.'

Robinson indicated he was finished.

'Would you like some coffee?' Mary asked.

'Splendid idea,' Robinson said, opening the door to let her through.

'No joy with Rafferty?' Robinson asked.

'He obviously knows something, but I really think this is some maverick action. He called his solicitor, you know. Talked to him for at least an hour.'

'Who was that?'

'Some weasel named Boyd. I've heard the name, haven't run across him before.'

'We've applied for permission to put a tap on Rafferty's phone. I doubt he'll be careless enough to use it, but you never know. The Commissioner has spoken personally to every newspaper editor, the television and radio chiefs. They promised full co-operation. I have thirty detectives out on the streets making enquiries. We should have something from them this morning. They're interviewing everyone on the bus, outside the school, local shopkeepers. Someone must have seen what happened.'

Robinson bent down to pet the dog as it wandered into the living room. Carney watched in disgust as the dog rolled over on its back, the back legs kicking as Robinson tickled its stomach.

Co. Armagh, Saturday June 16th

Graves could not think straight. They refused to let him sleep. It seemed to him ironic that a few hours earlier he had been begging for some signs of life from his captors, and now all he wanted was peace to sleep.

They rattled the cat flap, banged on the walls, switched the light on and off and, worst of all, he could hear them talking at the door, the conversation low enough to be unintelligible.

Although he knew they would come eventually, come when they judged the time to be right, he felt it was all rather pointless. After all, what could he tell them that was worth all this? The only name he knew was that of Crowe. His job was to safeguard the weapons, hand them over and disappear.

What a waste of effort, he thought, watching the cat flap swinging noisily on its hinges.

Celbridge, Saturday June 16th

Sinead woke to the sound of a thin whistle emanating from somewhere downstairs. Her mouth was dry and her throat was sore. This morning everything was crystal clear. She had been on her way to the bus stop when the man jumped out of the car. The heavy bag had held her arm back as she tried to hit him. She recalled being dragged by her hair and pushed face downward, an arm or a heavy object pressing into the base of her spine. A sharp stabbing pain at the top of her leg had been followed almost immediately by a drowsy feeling. She remembered little after that.

The whistling abruptly stopped and was replaced with the sound of rattling crockery. She lay very still, her breathing shallow and tentative, goose pimples creeping up her arms as footsteps sounded on the stairs.

Her growing apprehension faded when the man nudged the door open with his foot. She had imagined her captor as some sort of monster, drooling and slavering from a mouth full of hideous fangs. Instead, the man who released the straps from her arms seemed quite ordinary and when he smiled and said 'good morning' the tenseness across her stomach eased. His blue, woollen sweater needed darning and it was clear from the thick stubble on his chin that he had not yet shaved.

Holding the cup steady in both hands she took a sip and started to cough as the liquid caught in her throat. Boyle lifted her up and wedged two pillows behind her back. She watched him warily as he sat on the edge of the bed, casually drinking the sweet tea.

'Who are you?' she asked, fighting hard to control the tremor in her voice.

The man looked mildly surprised. 'It's not important,' he said, sipping again from the cup.

'You're in big trouble,' Sinead said. 'My father's an inspector.'

'Yes. I know. That's the whole point of the exercise.'

'What do you want from him?'

The man leaned forward, peering into her cup. 'Finished?'

She resisted as he tried to fix the straps back on her wrists. His reaction was to apply a steady pressure and they hovered for a moment like two arm wrestlers straining for advantage. Sinead gave in with a cry.

'Best not,' the man said, before gathering up the cups and leaving her alone once more.

A few minutes later she heard a door close downstairs, followed by a car starting up. The noise of the wheels crunching over gravel drifted up to her room, then the car accelerated away, the sound fading gradually into the distance.

Dublin, Saturday June 16th

Mary gave a start when the phone rang. Carney held the palms of both hands in front of him. They let it ring five times.

Mary took a deep breath. 'Hello,' she said.

'Good morning, Mrs Carney,' the voice said. 'I haven't much time, so listen very carefully. Your daughter is well and will remain so as long as you do exactly as I say. Your husband knows what this is all about, so the message will make sense to him. He has someone and we want him. What I propose is a simple swap. We're willing to exchange your daughter. I'll phone same time tomorrow for his decision. If he needs any encouragement, tell him that if the answer is "no", I'll start sending you pieces of your daughter through the mail.'

Mary stifled her scream. 'Listen . . .' she began to say as the line went dead.

Brendan Rafferty paced the living room, his arm in a sling. Callaghan was in the kitchen talking to Rose and Charlie sat impassively, his eyes following a man with a plastic bag who was extracting the spent bullets from the wall with a pair of tweezers.

As the officers moved away, their work finished, Rafferty calmed down, taking a bottle of scotch from the table and pouring himself a generous measure.

'All we saw,' Callaghan said, 'was this guy with a limp, hopping into the driver's seat. He threw something over his shoulder into the back, presumably the gun. He shot off down the road. It was over in a few seconds. Look, I told you all this last night, after it happened.'

Rafferty stood up and resumed his pacing. 'The whole world's gone mad. That cretin of yours has gone off half cock and kidnapped Carney's daughter, some lunatic tries to blow me away, for God knows what reason, the Gardai are all over the place . . . Christ!'

Callaghan took out a handkerchief to wipe his face. 'He was supposed to kill Jockey,' he moaned, wishing he was back in Waterford, minding his own business.

'Did you give them a description of the man?' Brendan asked, halting at Callaghan's chair.

'Yes,' Callaghan said. 'I gave them a description. What are we going to do about Boyle?'

Brendan paused in his wanderings. 'Do? I know what I'm going to do. Nothing. This was not what I hired him for. What you do is your business. If I were you I'd keep clear of Carney. Well clear.'

Charlie nodded his head in agreement. 'I don't think he's pleased,' he said.

Fitzgerald showed the two detectives to Carney's office, pausing at the door, waiting to see if his presence was required.

Carney shook his head, allowing the Sergeant to leave. 'I hear you have something for me?' he said when the two men were seated comfortably.

The officer with the shock of fair hair acted as spokesman, pulling a well-worn notebook from the top pocket of his jacket. 'I don't know how much Superintendent Walsh told you on the phone.'

'He didn't tell me anything. I received a note from the Murder Squad saying you had further information concerning Brendan Rafferty.'

'That's correct,' the fair-haired man replied. 'Late yesterday afternoon, someone tried to kill Rafferty. Apparently a man drove up to the house and opened fire with an automatic weapon. The forensic boys have analysed the cartridges and confirm that they came from a Russian-made rifle. Witnesses at the scene gave a description of the man which tallied with a wanted notice originating from your office.'

The officer passed the notebook to Carney.

'Sergeant Fitzgerald,' Carney called as he read the description of the limping assailant. 'Get onto Special Branch with this. I think Mr Crowe is back in town.' He leaned back in his chair and sighed. What a pity I've got other important things on my mind right now, he thought.

Mary Carney rubbed the dish over and over again, unable to think straight or keep at peace. Brian stood by her side, holding another plate ready to be dried, afraid to bring it to his mother's attention.

It was like a dream, something that happened to other people in the newspapers, something you read about, shook your head and thanked God it had nothing to do with you.

The suppression of the incident in the press and on the television had been a relief at first, but now she felt cheated. There was no one outside the family and the force to share it with and it was becoming unbearable. Everyone was acting so normally. All she wanted to do was to retreat to a corner of the house and scream and never stop. At times she could hardly bear to think of what had happened, the possible consequences too horrible to contemplate. To blot it out of her mind was the only way she felt she could stay sane, yet at the same time she felt she was letting her daughter down. It was unfair that Sinead had all the terror to face, it was all so unfair.

Brian put his arm around his mother's shoulders, gently taking the dish from her hand. He led her into the lounge and sat her down by the window.

'Dad'll get her back,' he said, holding her tight. 'You'll see.'

The street was deserted as Carney and Fitzgerald stepped out of the car. The door to the disco was open and an overfull dustbin sat at the entrance to the stairs. 'Doesn't look as if Callaghan is here,' Fitzgerald said.

The door to the bar was open, the sound of glasses clinking in the sink competing with music from a portable radio on the counter.

Maeve caught the movement outside as she placed the glasses in the drying rack.

'Hello!' she called, emerging from the back room with a dish cloth in her hands.

'Where is he?' Carney asked.

Maeve tossed the towel over the door handle. 'He went out yesterday afternoon. I haven't seen him since.'

'Does he often do that?' Fitzgerald asked, turning off the radio.

'He never tells me where he's going or what he's doing.'

'It's urgent we speak to him,' said Carney.

'He's not involved, is he?' Maeve asked suddenly.

Carney ignored Fitzgerald's glance. 'We have reason to believe he is.'

'I don't believe it,' she said. 'He just wouldn't do anything like that. Look, I was sorry to hear about your kid but I know he wouldn't stand for anything like that, he really wouldn't.'

'Did he say where he was going . . . mention a name . . .?'

'He didn't say. That goon of Rafferty's came for him, there was a bit of an argument. I heard Brendan Rafferty's name mentioned. I assume he went to see him.'

'And didn't come back?' Fitzgerald asked.

'Not unusual,' said Maeve.

'Who told you about my daughter?' Carney asked.

'That man . . . Charlie, I think they call him.'

'I remember Charlie,' Carney said. 'Thought he'd retired. Where can I find him?'

Maeve looked doubtful. 'Don't know where he lives, but he sometimes hangs out in Mooney's Bar off O'Connell Street. I've seen him in there a few times. If he isn't there now, they might know where you can find him.'

'We should lift the whole bloody lot of them,' Fitzgerald said, as they sat in the snarl of traffic in Parnell Square. 'We could lift them on suspicion of withholding evidence.'

'I don't think it would do much good,' Carney replied. 'I know how these people operate. Rafferty and Callaghan are too smart to be directly involved in something like this. I think they planned to get Jockey. Most likely they used their own boys. When the hit on the ambulance fell through, someone felt his head was about to roll and went off half cocked. You saw Rafferty. He was worried sick. Sick enough to call in a solicitor to handle it for him. Boyd obviously thought Rafferty's involvement was tenuous enough to deny it outright. What does Rafferty do? He sends Charlie after Callaghan. Callaghan has to have some knowledge of what happened.'

'You don't really think Callaghan had anything to do with setting this up?'

'No. But he might know the man responsible.'

Celbridge, Saturday June 16th

Sinead propped herself up on one elbow, holding her face close to the bowl of soup, her movement restricted by the strap still attached to her right wrist. Boyle sat on the edge of the bed watching her. She had heard him return an hour ago, had heard him working in the kitchen. A packet of biscuits lay open at the bottom of the bed and she guessed that they constituted all she would have in the way of solid food.

His constant gaze annoyed her and she tried to pretend she was alone, determined not to speak unless he spoke first. When the soup was finished, she slid the bowl to the side of the bed, turning her back to him.

'I spoke to your mother this morning.'

Sinead turned her face towards him. 'What did she say?'

'She wants proof you're still alive.'

'Why didn't you let me speak to her?'

'I can't take you with me.'

'I could write her a letter.'

'Too risky. The Gardai would check the postmark. I'd have to travel miles to throw them off the scent and I wouldn't want to leave you here alone for too long.'

Sinead began to lose interest in the conversation.

'I could send her something of yours,' Boyle continued. 'I could send her one of your fingers. The doctors have ways of telling that it was cut from living flesh.'

CHAPTER TWENTY NINE

Co. Armagh, Saturday June 16th

The cell door flew open, heavy boots clattered over the concrete floor and arms lifted him to his feet. Graves felt himself being dragged forward, the table and chairs a blur as he sped past.

'Move! Move!' a voice screamed in his ear.

He tried to stand upright, digging his feet hard against the floor but the pull became stronger and he stumbled.

'Up! Up!' the voice yelled.

The room they transferred him to was much bigger but just as sparsely furnished. A single chair sat in the middle of the floor, wrist and ankle straps built into the arms and legs. A small stool lay behind the chair and in the corner was a large wooden crate, the top lying against the wall.

The hands beneath his arms moved to his shoulders and thrust him into the chair. His hands and feet were fastened, the leather manacles biting into his flesh. Before he could recover his senses the door slammed shut.

'Martin Graves?' a voice said from somewhere behind him.

He tried to answer but the words stuck in his throat.

'Doesn't want to co-operate,' a second voice said.

'Very poor attitude.'

'Let's give him one more chance.'

'Are you Martin Graves?'

Graves nodded.

'What's that supposed to mean?' the first voice rasped in his ear. 'I think he's trying to take the mickey out of us. Thinks he's a comedian.'

A flurry of blows rained down on his head and back. 'This won't do at all,' one voice said. 'We're going to have to stop being nice to him. Name?'

'Graves.'

A hand slapped the back of his head. 'Graves what?' the voice snapped.

Graves could not think fast enough. 'Graves, sir,' the voice informed him. 'Showing disrespect. Won't do at all.'

'Graves, sir.'

'Better,' the voice said.

'Now then, Mr Graves. I hear you've been a bad boy. A very bad boy indeed. A little bird tells me you've been carrying arms over the border, weapons that would be used to kill British soldiers. Bit of a hero, are you? Laid a few ambushes in your time, I'll bet. Toast of the town.'

Graves dropped his head. He had been stupid to think he could escape by giving them a name. Perhaps they already knew his history. It dawned on him that they would keep this going for days, no matter what he told them, and he felt a lump come to his throat.

'How many have you killed?' the voice asked. 'Two? Three? Ten?'

The uniformed man bent over the box, extracting a coil of wires. 'More than that?'

Dublin, Saturday June 16th

Carney and Fitzgerald surveyed the bar, squinting as they peered through the subdued lighting. Fitzgerald took a step back, glancing down the stairs.

'Not open yet down there,' he informed Carney.

'Excuse me,' Carney said to a passing waiter. 'We were supposed to meet a friend here. Fellow named Charlie. Has he been in?'

The waiter hesitated a moment. 'Old Charlie Ryan?'

'That's the man.'

'Not so far tonight. He should be in later. Never misses.'

Carney rubbed his hands together. 'We'll wait,' he said, ushering Fitzgerald towards the bar.

'Wouldn't mind at all.' Fitzgerald didn't wait for Carney's offer. They sat over in a corner, away from the main bustle.

'You think Charlie knows what's going on?' Fitzgerald asked after sipping from his pint of Smithwicks.

'Doubt he has a clue what the hell's really happening,' Carney replied, 'but you can bet your life he'll talk about it.'

'What makes you so sure?'

'He's stupid,' Carney said.

'Might not make much sense,' Fitzgerald warned.

'Doesn't really have to. If we can convince Callaghan we know exactly what happened I think we can get him to talk.'

Ten minutes later, the waiter directed Charlie over to their corner. It took a few seconds for Charlie to recognise them and sense danger, but before he could react, Carney had taken him by the arm and invited him to join them.

'Charlie Ryan,' Carney said, shaking his head in disbelief. 'You know, Charlie, the nice thing about my job is the number of old friends who bob up from nowhere. What are you drinking these days? You know Sergeant Fitzgerald, Charlie. You must have met.'

Confusion clouded Charlie's features and he turned his head first to Carney, then to Fitzgerald, unsure of how to react.

'What are you doing with yourself these days?' Carney asked, waving his arm at the waiter. He ordered drinks and proposed a toast. 'To old times,' he said, raising his glass. 'Those were the days, Charlie. Old man Rafferty knew how to run a business. Professional from top to bottom. Nowadays . . .'

Charlie took a deep drink from the pint glass. 'Too impetuous, these youngsters,' Carney continued. 'Take Brendan for example. Quick temper, slow thinker. Not a good combination.'

Charlie nodded in agreement.

'You must notice a difference,' Carney suggested.

'Not the same,' Charlie answered after a little thought. 'Always blaming other people. No respect.'

'I know how it is,' Carney sympathised, patting him on the shoulder. 'Same in our line of work. They're so ambitious these days. Full of textbook knowledge but no real feel for the job. Always on the lookout for other people to blame.'

'I was only trying to help,' said Charlie.

'Things do go wrong,' Carney agreed. 'All the time. Kidnapped my girl, Charlie. Bad mistake, but they're too proud to admit it. They try to cover up, pretend it's nothing to do with them. Pass the buck to someone else and everything will be okay. Not the way old man Rafferty would have handled it. He corrected his mistakes.'

Charlie finished off the pint. 'Same again,' Carney called across the bar. 'Terrible thing to happen to a little girl. Do you know her, Charlie?' Carney pulled out a wallet from his inside pocket and took out a photograph. 'Taken last year,' he said, passing the picture over. 'Old Rafferty loved children. Looked after his. He'd turn in his grave if he knew what they'd done.'

'Bad mistake,' Charlie agreed.

'Always left to us old timers to sort things out. Thing is, where do we start looking?'

Charlie returned the photograph. 'Don't know where she is. Don't know where he's taken her.'

'Going to be difficult. I'll tell you something though. For all their ambition and new fangled ideas, they're not as smart as us, Charlie. We have the experience. Experience wins every time.'

'All a mistake.'

'Suppose Brendan's blaming it all on Callaghan.'

Charlie picked up his drink. 'Blames everyone but himself.'

'Typical. What do you think, Charlie? Who do you think's to blame?'

Charlie shook his head, staring into the dark liquid in the pint glass. 'I'm sorry about your little girl. Crazy man.'

Carney felt his stomach knot. 'Crazy man?'

'They shouldn't have anything to do with nutters.'

Fitzgerald leaned over, patting Charlie on the arm. 'Some sort of cowboy, is he? Someone Callaghan knows?'

'Worked at Callaghan's Disco. Callaghan introduced him to Rafferty.' Charlie began to giggle. The rheumy eyes flickered to life as he rocked backwards and forwards in the chair. 'Not so much a cowboy,' he wheezed. 'More like a Red Indian.'

'Red Indian?' Carney said.

'The freckles. And the red hair,' Charlie roared.

'Boyle.'

'You know him?' Fitzgerald asked Carney.

'A red moustache as well?' Carney asked, suddenly serious.

'Shaved it off.'

'But is it Boyle?'

Charlie wiped a tear from the corner of his eye. 'Who did you think it was?'

Celbridge, Saturday June 16th

Boyle picked up the morning paper from the floor and carried it to the mattress by the wall. Easing himself down, he placed his jacket under his head. He grinned as he thought of the girl's frightened eyes, knowing that she would be easier to handle from now on. For once in his life he felt he was in control of the situation. The Garda had no idea where he was, even Rafferty and Callaghan knew nothing of his plans. This was all his own work.

There was nothing in the paper about the kidnapping. He really had them where he wanted them. Without the public attention, without the prying eyes of some nosey neighbour, he had a better chance of remaining undetected.

The house was isolated and so was the link to the main road. He had a right to be at the house. The family owned it. For the past few days he had been telling the locals in the small pub of his plans to refurbish the premises, so no one would think it suspicious if they saw him driving in and out of the lane. He had covered everything.

Soon he could begin to enjoy himself.

Flicking idly through the pages, he thought of how grateful Brendan Rafferty would be when this was all over.

Dublin, Saturday June 16th

'We should tell Robinson and Walsh,' Fitzgerald said.

Carney checked his mirror and eased the car into the traffic before speaking. 'Not yet,' he said. 'We need more.'

Fitzgerald was not convinced.

'If we handle Callaghan right, we can get him to help us,' Carney explained. 'If we send the whole squad in, he's liable to clam up.'

Ten minutes later they were parked less than a hundred yards from the Rafferty house. 'There it is,' Carney said, pointing to Callaghan's station wagon.

'Do we go in and get him?'

'If we try to question him in Rafferty's presence he won't say a word.' Carney rolled the window down and took in deep breaths of fresh air. 'He has to come out sooner or later. We have all night.'

Co. Armagh, Saturday June 16th

The pain in Graves' arm was excruciating, as if a hundred red-hot needles were being twisted under his skin. He could feel the sweat pouring down his face, soaking his collar, and blood ran out of the side of his mouth where, despite the rubber plug, he had managed to bite his tongue.

A new man had entered the room and his tormentors departed without a word.

'I'm sorry about this,' a soothing voice said. 'I had no idea this was going on. Quite unnecessary. Would you like a cigarette?'

Graves raised his head and peered at the man through bloodshot eyes. The man was dressed in civilian clothes, a neat blue suit offset by a striped, grey tie. A set of gold cufflinks shone under the overhead light.

'I see they've taken down everything you said,' the man said as he studied a sheet of paper on the table. 'You mention this man, Crowe, quite a lot. In fact you mention very little else. Tell me all about Crowe.'

Graves allowed his head to sink forward once again onto his chest. 'I've told you all I know.'

'Perhaps if I asked the right questions, that would make it easier for you.'

The man placed a cigarette between Graves' swollen lips. As Graves inhaled, the man untied the strap on his left hand. 'There, that's better,' he said, like some kindly nurse.

'We know that Crowe is back in Ireland,' he said. 'We've known that for some time. What we don't know is exactly where. If you could tell us that we would be very grateful.'

'All I had to do was watch the guns.'

'Yes, yes. You keep saying that, but where did the guns come from? Who gave them to you? Where are they now? What were they going to do with them? Where did Crowe fit in? You see, there's an awful lot you still have to tell us.'

'I don't know the answers.'

'Let's take them one at a time,' the man whispered, leaning close to Graves. 'They'll be back soon.'

CHAPTER THIRTY

Dublin, Saturday June 16th

Callaghan dabbed a handkerchief at the trickle of blood running from the corner of his mouth.

'Let's start at the beginning,' Carney said, sitting sideways in the seat so that he was facing Callaghan. 'Where does Boyle live?'

Callaghan's mind raced. He nodded his head, trying to stall for time. Someone had talked. He saw no way of bluffing it out. If he denied all knowledge of it they would book him and, with Carney in this mood, probably half kill him as well. He knew he could expect no help from Fitzgerald. 'He lives with his sister. Dargle Road. I don't know the number. I think it's the third house from the end, off Shanganagh Road.'

'Okay,' Carney said, easing back in the seat. 'You have a choice. You can talk to us off the record or you can talk to Superintendent Robinson down at the station. If you tell us everything you know you can climb out of this car and go home. I can't make it more attractive than that.'

Callaghan took a deep breath. 'Could we drive away from here?' he asked, nervously peering out of the window at the Rafferty house.

'Give Sergeant Fitzgerald your keys,' said Carney. 'He'll move your car.'

They parked the two cars under a street light half a mile from the Rafferty house. The night had closed in quickly, relaxing Callaghan. His mouth had stopped bleeding, the pain now a dull throbbing.

'Boyle was to watch the hospital,' Callaghan told them in a whisper. 'Rafferty wanted a way to get at Jockey.'

'Kill him you mean?' Carney interrupted.

'I don't know anything about that.'

'How did Rafferty know that Jockey was being sent to Beechmount?'

Callaghan shrugged. 'Rafferty used to get these calls. I don't know who from. The word was that Jockey was being moved. That's all I know about it.'

Carney clicked his tongue against the roof of his mouth. 'That's not enough,' he said.

Callaghan looked first at Carney and then at Fitzgerald for inspiration. 'What more can I tell you?'

'You can tell us where Boyle is holding my daughter. You can tell us what the plan is. You could even tell us you'd like to help.'

'For God's sake, I don't know where he's holding your daughter. The stupid bastard did this on his own. He didn't tell anyone what he intended to do. He could have taken her anywhere. I don't even know what he hopes to achieve.'

'We're going for a little drive. Give you time to think. If at the end of it you can't come up with something better, I'm going to book you. I'm going to book Rafferty and I'm going to make sure you never see the light of day again. If anything happens to my daughter, you won't even see the inside of a court. Now sit back quietly and have a good think. You haven't much time left.'

Callaghan made up his mind. 'I think we can work something out.'

'What do you suggest?'

'I know Boyle's sister.' Carney raised his eyebrows. 'Met her a few times, that's all,' Callaghan said. 'It doesn't matter. I know her. I think she might be able to tell us where her brother is.'

'Dargle Road?'

Callaghan slumped back in the seat. God help me now, he thought, as Carney spun the car in a tight turn.

Co. Armagh, Saturday June 16th

'It seems odd to me,' the man in civilian clothes said as he read his notes. 'Right out of the blue, a man whose name you don't remember calls at your house, asks you if you want to earn a bit of money on the side, gives you a job of sitting in a derelict house in the middle of nowhere . . . Really. You can do better than that.'

Graves glanced nervously at the door.

'Let me tell you what I think actually happened,' the man continued, discarding the pieces of paper. 'I think you were part of a unit, headed by this man Crowe, which operated over the border. During one of your operations you were fired on by the army. Crowe was injured. Shot in the leg. He shipped out to Europe and the unit melted back into the community. A few weeks ago the man who called on you said the unit was reforming, that Crowe was back again and he had a job for you to do. You were to guard the weapons until Thursday morning. Then you were to deliver them to the unit. They were going to be picked up at six in the morning by a lorry, taken over the border and used indiscriminately to shoot voters at the European elections. That's what I think.'

Graves looked up in surprise, blinking hard as if he could not believe what he had just heard. His mouth fell open and he started to cough.

'You see,' the man informed him. 'We picked up the rest of the unit before they got to you. One thing that puzzled us . . . Crowe was missing.'

Graves felt nothing. His mind clouded over, shutting out the thought of why he had been put through all this if they knew more than he did.

'So you see. Your silence has served no purpose. My colleagues will be back any minute and there's still one important question to be answered. Help us on this and I can save you a lot of pain. Why didn't Crowe come up North and where is he now?'

Dublin, Saturday June 16th

The inside of the house was neat and tidy, chintz curtains hanging from a brass rod above the windows. A sideboard with gold-coloured fittings sat against the wall opposite the fireplace and a sofa and two chairs with deep, bucket seats formed an enclave in the centre of the room.

Boyle's sister sat nervously in one of the chairs, her hands clasped around her knees. She wore a pair of faded jeans and a white, frilly-necked blouse tied at the throat with a cameo brooch.

She constantly worried the brooch with her chin.

Callaghan sat in the chair next to her, his legs crossed, his arms resting loosely and dangling over the sides. He introduced Carney and Fitzgerald by their surnames and they nodded as they tried to relax on the sofa.

'We need to find Tony urgently,' Callaghan said. 'He was supposed to meet us this afternoon and he didn't show. It's very important.'

Ann Boyle shook her head to clear the red tresses of hair from her face. 'I haven't seen Tony for weeks. He was here about two weekends ago and that was the last time I saw him.'

'We've tried all the usual places and can't find him anywhere,' Callaghan explained.

'Why do you want him?'

'We have a job for him.'

'Not like Tony to turn down a job. Do you think something happened to him?'

'No, no, nothing like that,' Callaghan said. 'It's just that the job has to start tomorrow and we really need to get in touch with him tonight.'

'Does he have a girlfriend?' Carney asked.

'If he does, he keeps her very quiet. He had no close friends to speak of. He's a shy sort, my brother. Keeps very much to himself.'

'Did he mention going away anywhere?' Callaghan asked in desperation.

'He did phone me two or three nights ago. Said he had been thinking of working on the house and asked where the key was, but I know him, he has this notion every so often. Never gets round to it.'

'Which house is this?' Carney asked. 'I don't remember Tony being much of a handyman.'

'He isn't,' Ann replied, smiling. 'It's just talk.'

There was an awkward silence for a moment. 'You have another house?' Carney prompted.

'God, don't talk to me about it. Our uncle died, I think it must be seven or eight years ago now. He was a widower in his seventies. Left a cat, a dog, three budgies, a pile of debts and the house. How he ever lived in it I'll never know. Dirty, disgusting it was then and it's ten times as bad now. I wanted to sell it to pay off the debts, but Tony said no. He said he could get it fixed and we'd have a house in the country. Full of romantic ideas he was.'

'I'd love a house in the country,' Fitzgerald said, unfolding his arms. 'At least my wife would.'

Ann laughed. 'You can have this one if you want. If it's still standing.'

'Did you give him the key?' Carney asked.

'No need. There's a spare one lodged between two bricks. You won't find him there if that's what you're thinking. No one would stay a night in that dump.'

'Just thought he might have finally got round to doing it up. Decided to stay there. Is it far out?'

'Place called Celbridge outside of Lucan. Right in the middle of nowhere. Too far to walk to the nearest shops, nothing to do. What we'd use it for I can't imagine.'

Fitzgerald sighed. 'Sounds romantic. My wife loves the countryside. She loves those houses that have long, winding paths leading up to them. Does yours have one?'

'Sort of. It's what's at the end of it that counts as far as I'm concerned.'

'Suppose it doesn't have a telephone,' Callaghan said hopefully.

'You're joking. Besides I told you, it was just a notion of his. You won't find him there.'

'No harm done if we look,' Callaghan suggested. 'We can't find him anywhere else.'

'It's daft,' Anne said. 'You don't want to go running out there at this time of night. There's no electricity or water laid on. He'd come home even if he was working on it.'

'But he hasn't, has he?' Callaghan said, giving her knee a squeeze.

'He's hardly ever here. When he's not working all night at that disco of yours he's out at some night club. Don't know where he sleeps half the time. I assumed he slept at the disco.'

'He does sometimes,' Callaghan said, 'but I haven't seen him there for a few days. I think we'll nip over to the house and check. How do we get there?'

Outside Carney gave orders to Fitzgerald. 'Get hold of Robinson and Walsh. Tell them to meet us in my office in ten minutes and have Walsh alert the depot. I'm going to phone and check on Mary. Callaghan, you go home. Say nothing, do nothing, pretend this didn't happen.'

Callaghan sighed. 'Bloody right, I'll say nothing,' he said.

Celbridge, Saturday June 16th

Boyle held the needle and syringe in the air, depressing the plunger until the golden liquid squirted out of the hypodermic. The girl was on her back, sleeping.

He tiptoed over to the edge of the bed and placed the end of his thumb gently into position. Lifting the girl's skirt he slid the needle under the soft flesh at the top of her thigh, slowly driving the heroin along the vein. The girl made a noise and opened her eyes, twisting her neck round to stare into his face.

He smiled at her, watching as her eyes misted over. 'There, there,' he said, patting her on the leg. 'That didn't hurt, did it?'

CHAPTER THIRTY ONE

Dublin, Saturday June 16th
Maire Brady allowed the nurse to raise her up, letting her arms dangle loosely over the covers as three thick pillows were placed into position.

'You know who you look like?' the nurse asked, tucking the sheets under the mattress and smoothing down the coverlet. 'The invisible man. Remember that dishy blond-haired man who used to play the part in the television series? They wrapped his head in bandages. Personally, I thought it was a waste. Couldn't see that gorgeous face half the time.'

Maire lay back, wishing the nurse would go away. 'Sister says you're to have a bed bath. And she says she'd like you to try and walk a bit. Maybe tomorrow, tomorrow morning. You'll enjoy being on your feet again.'

Maire leaned over, her hand closing on the notebook and pencil. Since her second operation, it was the only way she could communicate, the crisscross of stitches along her jaw and chin making it impossible for her to move the muscles of her lower face.

She rolled sideways, supporting the pad on the bed, the spidery scrawl slanting down the page. The nurse took the note and smiled. 'You must be feeling better. Has your boyfriend been informed of your . . . accident?'

Maire increased the pressure on the slim pencil, forming the letters slowly.

'He's in the hospital?' the nurse said in surprise. 'What a pair you two will make. I'll have to ask the sister, but I'm sure she won't mind if I walk you over there in the morning.'

The nurse fussed over the locker, tidying the assortment of screwed-up notes. 'I won't throw these away,' she said. 'You can use some of them over again.'

Maire felt as if her body belonged to someone else, some sort of tortured shell that she had slipped into by mistake. Her memories of what it was like before she met Jockey were precious. Without them she knew she would not be able to survive. If she ever let go and returned to the physical wreck of a body that needed its daily doses of drugs to stay alive, she would go mad. She had to survive. Just long enough for her to have her revenge. If she could summon up the strength for that, her ordeal would have a purpose.

She closed her eyes to help her concentration, not opening them even when the nurse returned with the bowl of tepid water and a sponge.

Walsh and Robinson were both on the telephone, their conversations overlapping. Several officers hung about outside in the corridor waiting for orders. Fitzgerald was taking notes as Carney talked earnestly to him. A tray of sandwiches and coffee arrived almost unnoticed.

'I know this must be hard on you,' Robinson said, trying to make himself heard above the chatter. 'It's the safest way. If we go out there in a barnstorming fashion in the middle of the night, too many things can go wrong. First of all we're in unfamiliar territory. We don't know how the land lies, what cover there is, whether or not he's armed. There are too many questions unanswered for us to take even the slightest chance. We could end up with the thing we least want. A hostage situation.'

Walsh nodded his agreement. 'I don't think we could get into the house without alerting him. The doors will be locked and the first noise he hears, he'll make straight for your daughter. If we arrive before first light, we have time to put our men into position.'

Carney bit his lip. His instinct was to go in now, to snatch his daughter before the madman had a chance to do her any harm. The plan as it stood seemed a let-down after the initial rush of enthusiasm.

'It makes sense,' Robinson added. 'We know he's supposed to call your wife in the morning. We also know there isn't a phone at the house. He has to leave to make the call. The odds are he'll leave your daughter secured in the house. It would be too risky to ferry her back and forth every time he went out. It would be asking for trouble. When he's out of the house it'll be simple.'

Carney knew that it made sense. It was the thought of subjecting his daughter to Boyle's presence for a moment longer than was absolutely necessary that knotted the muscles in the pit of his stomach.

'These men have worked with me in similar situations,' Robinson assured him. 'They know what to do.'

Carney found himself nodding, but with no great conviction.

Co. Armagh and London, Saturday June 16th

The medic placed a stethoscope on the prisoner's chest, moving it slowly over the clammy skin. 'He can't take any more. You have to let him rest.'

Graves heard the words that could signal his salvation but they were meaningless. Pain seared every nerve-end of his body. The medic stepped to one side, allowing the civilian to take a close look at the prisoner. 'Has he said anything?'

'No, sir. Nothing at all.'

The civilian shook his head.

'Any more and you'll lose him,' said the medic.

'Okay. Get him to the hospital. I'll arrange a guard. When he's fit, I want him brought back here. Is that clear?'

The medic nodded.

Five hours later, the civilian was feeding pigeons in Trafalgar Square, a bag of corn resting on his lap. The usual crowd of tourists wandered about, taking pictures of Nelson's Column. The old Indian was there, his canvas bag sagging under the weight of birds fighting for the seed.

'It is pleasant for this time of year,' Hudek said.

'Exceptionally mild. My wife wants me to take a holiday. We have a cottage in Devon, near the beach.'

'That must be very nice.'

'It makes a pleasant change. And you? Do you miss Prague?'

'Prague is nice in the summer. Perhaps a little too hot. I prefer the lakes in Hungary.'

'Your information. It came too late.'

'Oh,' Hudek said, surprised. 'I heard on the radio that it was a success. A large find of arms it said.'

'Arms at the border are ten a penny. We missed Crowe.'

'That is too bad.'

'Why didn't you contact us when he made the deal? We could have followed him from the start.'

'As I told you. I was not aware of the deal until Crowe was back in Ireland. I contacted you as soon as I could.'

The pigeons scattered as a boy ran through the Square, his hand clinging tightly to a red balloon.

'My people are not very happy. We pay you to know.'

'It is unfortunate, but one of those things. Next time is always different. You must learn to take what you can and be grateful.'

'Another thing. How did Crowe get hold of the arms?'

'Through Amsterdam, I believe.'

'Amsterdam?'

'Not my department.'

By the time the pigeons had settled again, Hudek was alone on the bench. The deal had gone well. The Comecon Trade Association had much-needed hard currency, he had his commission and the British had their arms. More important, his reputation with all sides was intact. True, he had betrayed Crowe. But then, who was Crowe? No government supported him. Crowe was unimportant.

Dublin, Sunday June 17th

The convoy of cars parked along Harcourt Street, the Garda drivers standing by the passenger doors.

The city was quiet. A gentle breeze wafted mist around the whispering groups and several men had the collars of their jackets turned up to ward off the chill. A yellow glow fanned out from the building behind them, shadowy figures silhouetted against the windows of the upper floors.

Inside, the reception desk was manned by a young sergeant, his buttons gleaming in the overhead lights, a cup of steaming tea in his hand. Groups of men gathered and split up as instructions were passed on, and units left the building to join the drivers in the street outside.

Carney came downstairs ahead of Walsh and Robinson, joining Fitzgerald as he signed out in the book at the desk. They chatted at the door, their voices low.

'Won't be long now,' Fitzgerald said.

'You get some sleep,' Carney replied. 'I'll phone you when it's over.'

Making sure Robinson was out of earshot, Fitzgerald leaned closer. 'Shoot first. Don't take any chances.'

'I have a feeling they won't let me near the action,' Carney said, cutting him off. 'I have a feeling Robinson doesn't trust me.'

He paused at the door to survey the scene in the street. The lead car was already moving away, a plume of white exhaust leaving a trail along the kerb. He hurried out, ducking his head as he eased himself into the back seat of the third car, barely having time to settle before Walsh gave the order to move. They kept in close formation, no more than forty feet separating each car as they glided through the deserted streets and out onto the Lucan road. The trees rustled their leaves as the convoy sped past, ignoring traffic lights as it made its way purposefully into the night. The journey passed in silence, each man with his own thoughts and expectations.

As the car crunched to a halt on the winding country lane, Carney suddenly felt a sharp stab of dread in the pit of his stomach. A warning that the hardest part, the waiting, was about to begin.

The rear car blocked off the lane, red stop lights positioned well back from the arena of operations. Two Gardai stood watch on the road, their colleagues continuing on to join the others.

The house stood bleakly against the lightening sky, the crumbling chimneys jutting just above the trees. The rest of the building was hidden in the protective cloak of the oak trees. Four Gardai from the lead car stealthily made their way past the house, keeping close to the far side of the road. A further four, armed with semi-automatic weapons, took a position behind the ditch directly opposite the house.

Carney, Walsh and Robinson entered the field that ran up to the north wall of the building, the driver and another officer making a sweep that took them to a position at the rear. Fifty yards down the road, another squad of armed Gardai spread out along the ditch, their car hidden round a bend in the road, blocking any chance of escape. Walsh checked his watch and whispered into the pocket radio as he confirmed the time and positions of all the units.

Carney gazed at the dark building, wondering where his daughter was being held. From his spot behind a clump of small bushes he could see the back of the house with its crumbling facade. A rain barrel lay close to the steps leading up to what Carney assumed was the kitchen. The moon appeared briefly through the high clouds giving a brief, tantalising view of details of structure and Carney concentrated on committing them to memory. He knew the worst time would be when the sun rose above the horizon. They would have to wait, silently and patiently. The radio whispered at his side and Walsh gave the thumbs-up sign.

'They can see his car on the other side,' he announced with satisfaction.

There was no reaction from Carney. It had never entered his head that Boyle would be anywhere else. Robinson moved in a crouch to a rotting tree stump several yards closer, ducking down and testing the ground for cover. It was difficult to tell in the blackness how well concealed from view they would be when the sun rose over the fields.

'What do you think?' Robinson asked Walsh as he scrambled back to his original position.

'Hard to tell. I suggest we make doubly sure by moving back and having another look at it when it gets lighter. I doubt Boyle will be on the move before six.'

'I don't want to take any chances,' Robinson said. 'Tell all units to move back. We'll review it later. One thing that bothers me is if Boyle is the restless type. I hope the sod doesn't like wandering about at the crack of dawn.'

'We'll have to play it by ear,' Walsh said. 'No one moves without my say so.'

Robinson joined Carney by the bushes. 'I think he's probably holding her in one of the back rooms away from the road. Upstairs I should imagine. If it all goes to plan we just have to walk in when he leaves to make the phone call. If he changes his mind we should be looking for a way in at the back.'

'I think we should assume the back door's locked. I can just see a window . . .' Carney paused as the moon made a brief appearance. 'Not sure, but I think it's leaded. Can't see any ladders lying about the back.'

'There's a drainpipe at the far end, looks too far away from that back bedroom window.'

'Probably rotten,' Carney guessed. 'It's going to be difficult to storm the house and gain a quick entry.'

'Out of the question if we want to keep him separated from your daughter.'

Robinson moved towards Walsh. 'It's a real problem if our friend doesn't move.'

Walsh rolled onto his back, the radio balanced against his chest. 'Let's think this through. If the worst comes to the worst, what is he likely to do? He's going to grab the girl and use her as a shield. He's probably armed or can threaten her life in some way. The automatics will be no use for precision shooting.'

'We have Riley and Jackson for that. We need them on either side of the house.'

'The risk . . . If we let him leave, what then?'

'He's in a hopeless position. The threat is all he has, if he carries it out he knows he's gone.'

'I don't think I'd like to rely on logical thinking on his part. If the idiot was into that, he wouldn't have even considered this.'

Robinson glanced over to where Carney was lying. 'We'd better get it right,' he said.

The sky glowed red, then orange, throwing the house and surrounding trees into sharp outline. Noises encroached on the silence, the sound of cows lowing in a nearby field mixing with the hedgerow twitter of early-rising birds.

The men in the fields and lanes shrank back, fearful that they would be seen. They peered through stalks of grass, around hillocks and over the tops of cobwebbed leaves, watching for signs of life. As the sun rose in the sky, splitting the fragmented clouds with shards of gold, the tension grew.

Boyle was roused by a shaft of sunlight on his face. He blinked himself awake, his hand feeling on the floor for his cigarettes. He struck a match against the rough floorboards and walked to the window. The countryside was bathed in light, branches swaying gently in the breeze. Black and white cows wandered from the shelter of a chestnut tree to the open grass, lowing as they moved up the slope. Boyle stretched and scratched himself. Shuffling to the door, he stopped to pick up the pan, turning his nose up at the congealing soup.

The girl was lying on her side, the ropes twisted over her shoulder. She moaned softly as Boyle's shadow fell across the bed. Satisfied that she was still sleeping, he padded quietly down the stairs, shivering as he walked into the shaded kitchen.

Twisting off the top, he poured water from a plastic container over the remains of the soup, then topped up the water in the saucepan. The calor gas burned yellow, then with a roar enveloped the bottom of the saucepan in a fierce blue flame. Boyle did a quick calculation of the stores he needed for a few more days. He would buy them on his way back from Lucan, he thought, as he spooned coffee into two glazed mugs.

Running a Bic razor over his dry skin, he scratched away the night's growth of stubble. He carried the plastic container into the bathroom and poured the cold water carefully into the wash basin. The cold stung his cheeks and he massaged his face, patting himself dry with a tissue.

The water boiling in the pan brought him quickly to the kitchen. It hissed as it ran down the sides of the mug, blowing clouds of steam over his face. Sipping from one of the mugs as he walked, he made his way up the stairs to the back bedroom to serve breakfast.

'That's our man,' Robinson said.

Carney nodded, his eyes fixed on the spot where Boyle had made his brief appearance.

'The cover's better than I thought.' Robinson was pleased that all of the units were well hidden by the natural outline of the fields and trees. 'Once he makes a move for the car he's had it.'

Walsh crept cautiously towards them, his eyes scanning the house. 'Six forty,' he announced. 'He usually calls about nine. Give him half an hour . . . no, more like fifteen minutes, to lock up the house, drive to a phone . . . another two hours or thereabouts.'

Carney shut his eyes tight. Another two hours of this awful waiting, he thought, and I'll go crazy.

'Everything's quiet at the front. Riley and Jackson are in position but I'm worried about those bloody oak trees.'

'Can we put Riley and Jackson at each corner of the house instead of behind the hedge?' Robinson asked, craning his head for a better view.

'Too risky. I don't want their line of fire to be up and down the lane.'

The radio crackled to life. Walsh acknowledged the call, holding the slim, plastic case flat against his cheek. The message barely carried to Carney who was only a few feet away.

'Shit!' Walsh muttered, frowning. 'There's a farmer with a van load of milk churns heading up the lane.'

Boyle prodded the girl awake. She opened her eyes slowly, blinking in the light. When she saw him she cried out, twisting her body to the far side of the bed.

'There's gratitude,' Boyle said. 'After all I did for you last night.' He loosened the rope on her left hand and placed the coffee within reach, immediately stepping away in case she attempted to throw it over him.

The girl started to cry. 'I want to go home.'

'Already?' Boyle responded in mock surprise. 'But the fun's only just started.'

Growing bored when the girl continued to sob, he closed the door and headed downstairs.

He twiddled the tuner on the radio to find the station he wanted, settling back to listen to the seven o'clock news.

Whistling out of tune to a Neil Diamond song, he contemplated the day ahead, rubbing his hands in anticipation as he thought of all the new things he could do to the girl.

CHAPTER THIRTY TWO

Dublin, Sunday June 17th
'I suppose it will be okay,' the officer on duty said, looking at his colleague for confirmation. 'I did hear Inspector Carney say that she was his girlfriend.'

'I think it would do her good,' the sister confided. 'She's been very low since they brought her in. Just for a minute or two and we'll see how she reacts.'

'Very good, Sister. When will you bring her up?'

'I think I'll wait until the doctor has done his rounds. About nine thirty, I should think.'

Maire listened to the nurse with growing excitement. 'Only for a short while,' the nurse was saying. 'We don't want to overtax you.'

She lay perfectly still as the nurse tidied the sheets in preparation for the surgeon's visit.

'There,' said the nurse, standing back to admire her handiwork. 'That should do nicely. Don't you go twisting and turning after I'm gone or you'll get me into trouble.'

The tray came round, a staff nurse reading out the medicines from a typed list, a young student assisting.

'You have to dissolve it first,' the senior nurse explained, placing a straw in the glass. 'How are you today? Feeling better?'

Maire wished they would stop asking her stupid questions when they knew she was unable to reply. The nurse apparently did not expect an answer as she immediately switched her attention back to the list. Maire accepted the proffered glass, draining it as quickly as she could.

When they had left Maire managed to raise herself and inch her way over to the locker. She opened the drawer and took out a face cloth. Carefully unwrapping it, her fingers trembling slightly as she opened it out, she stared at the shiny double-edged razor blade. When she had spotted it in the bathroom last night, she knew it was a sign. It would all be worth it if she could only keep her nerve.

Celbridge, Sunday June 17th
'They've escorted him back to the farm,' Walsh said as he watched a beetle climbing up his leg. 'I've told them to keep a man on the gate. You never know.'

Carney changed position and wriggled his toes to ward off cramp.

'I know,' Walsh consoled him. 'It's playing bloody havoc with my circulation.'

The cloud thickened as the winds from the north west freshened. On the far horizon, Carney watched the front building up, dark masses of low cloud scudding in after their journey over the Atlantic.

'Shit!' Walsh said, following his gaze. 'That's all we need.'

Robinson waved his hand to attract their attention, his finger trained on the upstairs bedroom of the house. Carney shaded his eyes from the glare and caught a hint of movement.

'Busy little bugger,' Walsh said, taking another check on the time. 'You know, I don't think my bones are enjoying this very much.'

Thirty minutes later, Walsh was still complaining as the rain began to fall. It slanted in on the wind, driving hard over the three men as they huddled close to the roots of the bush.

'Would be in the wrong direction,' Walsh grumbled, stuffing the radio inside his coat.

Down the lane and in the surrounding fields and ditches, men were quietly protecting their guns from the rain. The dried mud began to break up, forming greasy pools under their feet. The sharpshooters tilted the peaks of their caps at an angle to divert the water from their faces. In the house across the road their potential target paced uneasily behind the grimy windows of an upstairs room, the change in the weather putting his nerves on edge.

CHAPTER THIRTY THREE

Dublin, Sunday June 17th

'You could do with a bit of make-up,' Nurse O'Brien said, helping Maire from the bed.

Her colleague giggled. 'Must say,' Nurse Lennon added, nudging her partner, 'you do look a bit peeky.'

The two of them started to laugh, Nurse Lennon self-consciously covering her mouth with her hand to hide the gleaming brace fitted across her top teeth. They stopped abruptly when they realised the noise might carry to sister's office.

Maire was not laughing. She was paying no attention whatsoever to the conversation aimed to cheer her up. She was summoning every ounce of energy to concentrate on the task ahead. The wound below her mouth was throbbing violently, her legs shook, tension knotted the muscles in her shoulders, but she was determined not to let the chance slip.

'Now what we'll do,' Nurse O'Brien informed her, 'is let you walk as far as the lift, then we'll give you a ride in the wheelchair.'

Maire clung to the nurse's arm, gradually easing her grip as she gained in confidence. As long as she kept moving, she would be all right. She repeated the phrase to herself, *keep moving, keep moving . . .*

Nurse Lennon pushed the wheelchair along the corridor, slightly ahead of the others, punching the lift button as she checked the overhead indicator. 'Won't be long,' she told them. 'Are you okay?'

'In you get,' Nurse O'Brien said, as the lift doors opened. 'Now you sit down and relax. We'll deliver you in style.'

On the top floor, they swivelled the wheelchair into the corridor, the two nurses waving to the Garda on duty.

'This way, ladies,' he called, rising to greet them. 'Wheel her in.'

Nurse O'Brien fussed with the blanket over Maire's knees. 'You have your notebook and pencil?' she asked as she positioned the chair at the side of the bed. 'You two behave yourselves, no funny business.'

Jockey stared at the crumpled form swathed in bandages. 'Maire?' he asked, hardly able to believe it.

'Maire Brady herself,' Nurse O'Brien answered for her. 'Now you take care of her. We'll be just outside the door if you need us.'

Jockey watched with morbid fascination as the bandaged figure scrawled a message on the notepad, flinching when the white, bony arm extended towards him.

He accepted the piece of paper warily. HELLO JOCKEY. HOW ARE YOU?

'I'm fi . . . fine,' he stuttered.

He could just see her eyelids flickering in the darkness of two downward slanting slits. The nose was covered except for a gash of about an inch, the rest of her head completely enveloped, the bandages disappearing below the high neck of her nightdress.

Another note appeared in his hand. I'VE MISSED YOU.

Jockey began to feel uncomfortable. He had no illusions about his relationship with Maire. He knew what it was that had kept her with him and he realised what he had done to her.

'Missed me,' he said woodenly, suddenly wondering what this was all about.

I HAVE SOMETHING FOR YOU.

Jockey frowned, his eyes fixed on her lap as she extracted a face cloth from the pocket of her hospital dressing gown. He studied her movements, mesmerised as the cloth was neatly unfolded. At first he thought it was empty, just a simple white cloth, edged with a blue border.

Even when the hand reached down, delicately feeling for the razor blade, the danger did not register. The first slash produced a thin red line from his ear to the base of his throat. He blinked once, his dazed expression fading as a second sweep of her arm severed his jugular vein. He tried to scream but the sound would not come. Instead there were funny gurgling noises and a burning in his throat. A river of blood soaked his shoulders and his limbs began to twitch. As he drifted into unconsciousness he caught a glimpse of a figure, dappled red, swaying over him.

The two nurses and the officer chatted in the corridor. The girls were letting themselves go, all the frustrations and tensions of the ward forgotten in the freedom of the top floor.

Maire stood in the doorway several seconds before she attracted their attention. The Garda jerked clumsily to his feet. Someone screamed and ran to the lift. The officer put out his hand towards the blood-soaked girl. Maire held out the note, her arm surprisingly steady.

I'M READY TO GO BACK NOW, the officer read, his lips moving silently.

Celbridge, Sunday June 17th

Boyle rinsed the steel comb in the remains of the water in the saucepan, shaking it once before running it through his head of thick, red curls. He used the kitchen window as a makeshift mirror, ducking this way and that to catch a glimpse of his reflection.

When he was satisfied, he slipped the comb into his back trouser pocket and checked his wallet. Doing a quick mental calculation, he estimated he had enough money for food and cigarettes to last him just under a week. Not that he expected it to drag on that long. The Gardai had no choice. They had been made an offer of blinding simplicity – an inspector's daughter for a piece of worthless scum.

Whistling softly, he pulled his tie from the door handle, fastening it with the embroidered motif nicely centred. With his jacket over his shoulder he made a final check that the girl was securely fastened and then bounced down the stairs to the front door.

Walsh was the first to react. 'All units ready,' he whispered into the radio, his body tensed for action.

Boyle closed the door, testing it with his shoulder to ensure the lock had caught. He paused on the low step, looking up at the sky. The rain had eased and the sun shone through the clouds, casting faint shadows over the garden. Boyle took his jacket in his left hand, his free arm feeling for the inside of the sleeve.

Robinson raised the megaphone to his mouth.

Boyle hesitated, one arm in the jacket. He patted the pockets, cursing under his breath when he realised he had left his cigarettes on the kitchen table. He fumbled in his pockets for the key, finally locating it caught in the teeth of the steel comb. Inserting it in the door he froze for a split second as the voice called for him to halt. With a reflex action he turned the key and launched himself against the door.

The ditches and hedgerows disgorged their complement of men. Carney vaulted the low bushes at the side of the house and gained a yard on Walsh, his legs pounding the slippery earth to the front step. The door slammed in his face and he heard Boyle racing up the stairs.

Windows were being smashed and men swarmed through the jagged holes, fanning out, searching the downstairs rooms. Carney followed them, overturning chairs as he pushed his way to the front of the column. At the top of the landing he heard a muffled scream from the bedroom to his right. With his leg at right angles to his body he levered himself forward off the wall, his foot splintering the panel of the door. Two more kicks and the wood shattered completely.

Boyle was on the bed, lying across Sinead, his hands frantically snatching at the one remaining rope on her right wrist.

He slashed at the rope with a carving knife, turning as Carney threw all his weight on top of him. He tried to stab downwards with the knife, but his wrist was caught in an iron grip and smashed against the post of the bed. With his free arm swinging, Carney rained blows on the side of Boyle's face. Boyle cried out, his body heaving. Sinead screamed as the men wrestled on top of her, her legs thrashing as she tried to haul herself free. Carney increased the tempo of the blows, feeling Boyle's teeth breaking. Hands and arms intervened and he heard voices shouting in his ear.

Three men held Boyle on the bed while the handcuffs were snapped to his wrists. Carney cradled Sinead in his arms, holding her head to his chest. As Boyle was roughly hauled to his feet, their eyes met and Boyle began to smile. Blood trickled from his parted lips as he lunged towards Carney.

'You lost,' Carney said.

'Ask your daughter what she lost. Ask your daughter how she enjoyed herself last night.'

Carney's face froze in a mask. The Gardai holding Boyle hesitated.

Boyle spat out a tooth. 'We're evens now.'

Carney let go of his daughter, his face turning scarlet. His arm went back, his hand clenching.

As he was about to launch himself at the grinning face, Robinson stepped between them. 'Get him out of here,' the Superintendent shouted. 'Get the bastard out of here.'

CHAPTER THIRTY FOUR

Dublin, Tuesday June 19th

Despite two days off and an unprecedented nine hours of sleep the previous night, Carney felt more weary than ever. The headache that had appeared on Sunday persisted, despite liberal doses of analgesics.

What he needed, he thought wryly, was a holiday. The irony of the situation made him smile for the first time since the incident with Boyle. It was impossible for them to leave Sinead on her own after the terrible experience. Since his daughter's release from hospital, she had followed Mary everywhere, into the kitchen, the garden, afraid to let her mother out of sight for a minute. Carney was sleeping in Sinead's room so his wife and daughter could be together.

'Morning. Nice to have you back.'

Carney looked up from the papers on his desk and waved for Fitzgerald to come in. 'Make some coffee, would you?'

'How's Sinead?'

'Physically, not too bad. Mentally, God knows. I've spent the last two days talking to assorted shrinks at the hospital. Enough to drive anyone crazy. I'm beginning to think that psychiatry is on a par with astrology. All bloody mumbo jumbo.'

'And Mary?'

Carney brushed a strand of hair from his face. 'A bit better. She was pretty shaken up by the kidnapping. I'm sure she thought we were going to lose Sinead. The fact that we got her back alive seemed to soften the blow of what Boyle did to her.'

'What about the press? I saw clips from the television news. It looked as if you were under seige.'

'They were all over the place. We even found one up a drainpipe trying to take photos of the bedrooms.'

'The court scene seemed nasty as well.'

'Usual reaction to child molesters.'

'Have you talked to Sinead about what happened?'

'The doctors told us not to. They prefer the victim to make the first effort. We'll have to face up to it sooner or later. She'll have to give evidence.'

Fitzgerald dumped an extra spoonful of coffee into Carney's mug. 'Perhaps it won't be necessary. A simple kidnapping charge would put him away for life.'

Carney accepted the coffee gratefully. The hot, black liquid revived him.

'What happens now about Rafferty?'

Carney groaned. 'I still can't believe it. They've transferred Maire Brady to the Caulder Mental Institution. Personally, I think she's probably a very sane young lady. It's her timing that's crazy. She did for Rafferty in a few seconds what his whole outfit and a raving lunatic couldn't achieve.'

'Have we nothing at all on him?'

'Nothing. Boyle's made a statement claiming he acted alone. Says he doesn't even know Rafferty.'

'That won't hold up.'

'We'll have to leave that side of it to Robinson.'

Fitzgerald was about to suggest a deal with Boyle when he caught himself just in time.

Crowe spent his time in the flat reading the newspapers from cover to cover. There was no doubt in his mind that the British Army had been tipped off. It was stretching credibility too far to believe that they had simply happened along at the right moment. They had picked up all but three of the men at the border. The weapons were gone and so was the cash. The only thing left was a slip of paper with the name and telephone number of a Libyan contact in London.

It would not be the first time he had to start from nothing. There was still an open line to his narcotic contacts and easy money to be made on the streets of every capital city in Europe. He could come back again. All that was needed was the will.

Sitting on the floor, his back resting against the wall, he wondered how long he could safely stay in Dublin. Behan was the only one who knew of his whereabouts and he had gone. He could trust no one, he decided. He would leave the country as soon as possible.

Dragging his battered suitcase from under the bed, he sorted through the tangled pile of clothing for his passport.

Rose Rafferty read the headline in the evening paper for the third time, unable to believe the reports of the kidnapping. She remembered her own youth, the relationship she had with her father. She remembered too the anger he had shown whenever she was hurt. She thought of how the Inspector must be feeling.

Sean had left for England that morning and she was to follow. The article in the paper did not mention Brendan by name, but the implication was clear to anyone with a knowledge of the drug trade in Dublin. As she sat in the chair, her knitting resting on her lap, the loathing for her brother-in-law reached a new pitch. If he had shown even a glimmer of regret she could have forgiven him. As it was, with Jockey dead, it was business as usual.

She folded the paper neatly, placing it on the table next to her plate, and went up to her room. Sitting on the corner of the bed, she lifted the mattress, feeling inside the slit down the side. Her hands closed over the shirt and she drew it out slowly, holding it to her cheek as she rocked to and fro.

As she ran her hands over the patches of dried blood, she began to sing. She had made up her mind.

Dublin, Thursday June 21st

Fitzgerald was waiting in the office when Carney arrived.

'Looking for promotion?' Carney asked.

'Couldn't leave without saying goodbye.'

Carney raised an eyebrow. 'They fired you?'

'Walsh seemed to think enough was enough. I go back on the desk today.'

'I'll miss you.'

'It's difficult . . . Look, I just wanted you to know. If there's anything I can do, or my wife, you only have to say the word.'

'I know. Thanks for the offer. I might have to take you up on that.'

'Problems?'

'Hard to say. Mary . . . well, I think she needs someone to talk to. Someone not connected directly. I thought perhaps your wife could call over.'

'She'd be delighted. Leave it with me. I'll get her to arrange it. I think women can handle these things better than we can.' Fitzgerald patted Carney on the arm. 'Oh, before I go. This came for you today.'

Carney took the parcel, turning it over in his hand. He tossed it on the desk while he took off his coat. It was wrapped in plain brown paper, the address written in block capitals. The edges were stuck with glue and a piece of string had been tied around the middle.

Carney checked the postmark. The ink was smudged, the lettering in the roundel illegible. He slit the flap with a penknife, tilting the parcel and giving it a shake. The shirt fell to the desk.

Laughter came from the corridor as two Gardai passed the open door. The rumble of traffic drifted up from the street below. Carney reached for the note, pinned above a patch of blood on one of the sleeves. The letters were in black pen, a stark announcement that made Carney's hands tremble. BRENDAN RAFFERTY – SLAUGHTERHOUSE 9.